www.HarperLin.com

Food Festival and a Funeral

A Pink Cupcake Mystery Book 3

Harper Lin

This is a work of fiction. Names, charac-
ters, organizations,places, events, and in-
cidents are either products of the author's
imagination or are used fictitiously.

Food Festival and a Funeral
Copyright © 2016 by HARPER LIN. All
rights reserved.

ISBN-13: 978-1987859386
ISBN-10: 1987859383

Contents

Chapter One

"How does this look?" Amelia asked, turning her computer screen toward her seventeen-year-old son, Adam.

"*Baker's Dozen. One makes all the difference*," Adam read aloud. "That actually sounds kind of good, Mom."

Amelia twisted her lips exaggeratingly.

"Kind of good? I wouldn't say it's Hemingway, but it's certainly better than that Brown guy and all his drivel."

"Who?" Adam asked, looking up from his math book.

"No, please don't tell me you don't know who Hemingway is. I'll go in the garage right this minute, start the engine, and sit in the car with the door shut if you tell me you don't..."

"I know who Hemingway is. *Farewell to Arms. For Whom the Bell Tolls.* Who is the other guy?"

Amelia pretended to wipe sweat from her forehead.

"Brown? He's nobody. Best you don't waste your time just to find out I was right, as I usually am."

She reached over her laptop and grabbed her coffee mug that proclaimed she was the World's Greatest Mom. Loudly, she sipped her hot tea.

"Whatever you say, Mom."

"But it looks good, right?" She tapped the computer screen.

"Yeah." Adam grinned as he nodded. "I'll read it when I'm done with my homework."

"You know, I wouldn't have ever dreamed in a million years that in addition to The Pink Cupcake I'd be updating my own social media outlets. See? Social media outlets? Don't I sound like I know what I'm doing?"

"You *sound* like you do," Adam said teasingly.

"Well, what I really mean to say is I couldn't have done it without you." Amelia set her mug down, reached over, and stroked her son's thick black hair. "I'm really proud of you, Adam. You've helped to make The Cupcake a success just as much as the cupcakes themselves have."

"It's no big deal, Mom." Adam shrugged, his cheeks getting red.

"What's no big deal?" Just then, Amelia's daughter, Meg, came bopping down the stairs from her room and into the kitchen.

"That Mom finally admitted you are adopted and I'm her favorite," Adam said to pester his sister. Meg rolled her eyes as she made her way to the refrigerator and yanked the door open.

"Hey, Mom. Did you know that there is a female cage fighter named Penelope 'Cupcake' Tate?"

"And why are you telling me about female cage fighters?" Amelia looked at her daughter as if she were suddenly growing a second nose on her forehead. "Please don't tell me it's a possible career choice."

"No," Meg said as she pulled out two bottles of water and shut the fridge door. "Katherine was telling me about her. She watches cage fighting with her brothers. We thought it might be a good idea to get her to endorse your cupcakes. Get it? 'Cupcake' Tate loves The Pink Cupcake. Cute, right?"

"Adorable. Except sports endorsements cost a lot of money. I think we'll have to wait a little while longer before we are big enough for that." Amelia smiled.

Meg shrugged again and went back upstairs, where she and her best friend, Katherine, were creating the marketing strategy for The Pink Cupcake in between diagraming sentences for English and finding out the value of "X" in algebra.

"Should I be worried Katherine is watching cage fighting and telling Meg about it?" Amelia looked at Adam.

"Naw." Adam shook his head, pulling his lips down in the corners.

Amelia finished typing a few more lines then, following the steps Adam had carefully written out for her, saved her new blog entry and with a couple clicks updated her website, Twitter, Facebook, and a few other outlets with her latest commentary on the beauty of baking.

She watched as her son quickly scribbled down equation after equation until finally he sat back, folded up his homework, stuck it in between the pages of his book, and slammed it shut.

"Done." He sighed, stretching his arms over his head. "I'll have your Gary-Fest feature up on the website by tomorrow."

"Right." Amelia exhaled, looking up at the ceiling. "I almost forgot about that." She let out a long, tired sigh.

"Aren't you looking forward to it?" Adam asked in surprise.

"I think the event itself will be good. But the city is making us pay double for the weekend just to be in the space we are in three hundred sixty-five days out of the year." Amelia huffed. "And if we wanted to settle in one of those prime pieces of real estate by the pond just for that weekend, my gosh, it's like handing over a down payment on a house. There's no way we could afford it."

"That's not fair," Adam replied.

"No, it isn't. It's politics."

"So what are we going to do?"

"I took the money from your college funds so I could keep The Pink Cupcake in her regular spot."

"I have a college fund?"

"Not anymore," Amelia teased as she stood from the table, took her cup to the sink, and rinsed it out.

It was aggravating as Amelia thought about the small fortune she'd had to hand over to the city just to participate in an event *they* thought up. *They* didn't operate the food trucks. *They* hadn't sunk their savings into a micro-business, losing sleep six out of seven nights a week figuring out how to stretch a dollar. But *they* sure did see a chance to make a few bucks off the people who did.

Choking down her disgust at her city's ground-level politics, she turned back to Adam.

"You plan on working? I think your sister and Katherine plan on helping out for a couple hours, passing out flyers and samples. It's all very glamorous."

"Sure. I'll take some pictures for you. Update your web pages. All that stuff." Adam cleared his throat. "Amy might come with, if that's okay."

Amy Leonard was the only girl Adam ever talked about. She was a neighbor, and even though the two teens tried to act casual and cool, it was obvious to anyone with eyes they liked each other.

They were cut from the same cloth. Amy skateboarded and wore weird T-shirts with words like SPOON or CLUNK on them that made sense to other people who were in the geek-realm but were incomprehensible to the rest of the world. Amelia had learned from Adam that Amy's parents had been together since high school.

Some people were lucky in love, was all Amelia could think. Every once in a while she might hear a loud "discussion" coming from their house. Other times she'd hear loud laughter. The Leonards seemed normal. Amelia was glad for that. The last thing she wanted was Adam's life taking a left turn in order to fill a hole left by divorce.

"Of course she can come. Tell her parents to come too. They can have cupcakes on the house."

"Great," Adam mumbled, trying to hide his smile. Letting out a deep breath, he scooped up his book bag and slung it over his shoulder while pushing himself up from the kitchen table.

"Leaving so soon?" Amelia pretended to look disappointed. She knew Adam was heading to his bedroom in the basement to text Amy about the upcoming Gary-Fest event. It was all so exciting.

"Is it really true that you had to dip into your savings to pay for your regular spot at the food fest?" Adam asked while hanging in the doorframe.

Amelia felt a twinge of guilt for telling him. The kids were good about money. They never asked for anything out of the ordinary when they easily could have. The life they'd all enjoyed while Amelia and her ex-husband, John, were still together had offered a lot more material stability. Designer shoes, the latest gadgets, dinners out almost every other night. Of course, John was having dinner with Jennifer now, his twenty-something girlfriend that he'd left Amelia for. Come to think about it, the meals weren't that great.

But now it was different. In her house, coupons were cut, pennies were pinched, and the threat of the car breaking down or the refrigerator crapping out would mean noodles with butter for dinner for a week.

"It isn't all that bad," Amelia lied. "We had it in savings. I just hate to part with it." She winked at Adam, who nodded.

"Well," he said, "if you ever need it, I've got money I've been saving. It's just a couple hundred dollars. I was saving for a car, maybe, or a trip to Las Vegas or something."

Amelia felt the sting of tears in her eyes, but after the divorce, she had made a promise to herself that she'd cried enough. Biting her tongue, she smiled at her son, who became more and more of a man every day.

"And a trip to Las Vegas is such a wise decision for a seventeen-year-old boy. Thank you, Adam. But no thanks. We're good." She tilted her head to the left as Adam gave her a nod and went down the stairs, pulling the door closed behind him.

Amelia quickly turned to the faucet, filled her mug with water, and took a big gulp. It helped push the tears back and just in time. She heard Meg and Katherine giggling and chatting as they made their way down the stairs toward the kitchen.

"Hi, Mrs. Harley." Katherine waved as the two girls took a seat at the kitchen table. "Did you hear about that killing in Florida?"

Chapter Two

Amelia gave Katherine a puzzled look while slowly shaking her head back and forth.

"Someone kidnapped some guy, and they found him stuffed in a suitcase, but the weird part..."

"There's a *weird* part?" Amelia interrupted her, looking at her daughter then back to Katherine.

"Yeah." Katherine nodded enthusiastically. "His feet were nowhere to be found. Why would anyone keep someone's feet? Hands I could see because, well, fingerprints and maybe even the head, but..."

"Katherine, honey, is your brother on his way?" Amelia interrupted again.

"Yeah." Katherine smiled. "He just called. Should be here in about ten more minutes."

"Okay." Amelia nodded, smiling. "How about a quick snack before they get here?"

Both girls agreed that was a stellar idea and continued their own conversation about an upcoming school project that they were partnered up for. It was some kind of history presentation, and the two girls thought dressing up as people from another era would be good. They discussed other parts of the project that Amelia didn't quite understand because both girls had the uncanny ability to talk and listen to each other simultaneously.

Without missing a beat, they devoured a small plate of oatmeal raisin cookies just before the horn of Katherine's brother's car could be heard honking in the driveway.

"You know, you can tell your brother he is welcome to come in. He doesn't have to stay in the car and honk," Amelia suggested, smoothing Katherine's hair as she passed by on her way to the door.

"Eww, yuck. It's bad enough I have to be seen driving with him. I don't want him infiltrating my friend zones, too." She wrinkled her nose. "Bye, girl!" She waved to Meg. "Bye, Mrs. Harley."

She stepped out the front door to her brother honking the horn again. Meg and Amelia laughed as they heard her yelling at her brother right before the car door slammed shut, and the sound of the engine faded away.

"Did you guys finish your homework?"

"Yup," Meg replied while heading back into the kitchen.

"What would you like for supper? I was thinking scrambled eggs and bacon."

"And pancakes?" Meg suggested with eyes wide.

"Sure."

"That sounds good." Meg loitered around the kitchen, looking at her fingernails, then at the ceiling, then lazily flipping through some sales papers on the counter.

"Something on your mind?" Amelia asked.

Meg took a deep breath and looked at her mother.

"Yeah."

"Is it a sit-down-and-brace-myself something or is it a keep-doing-what-I'm-doing-and-just-listen something?" Amelia watched her daughter's face.

"You can stay standing and just listen," Meg replied. Amelia saw her daughter's expression and felt a tug in her heart. Something was bothering her. A million scenarios went through Amelia's mind. Was she in trouble? Was she hurt? Did someone say or do something to her? Drugs? Alcohol? Or worse...dating?

"Do you like Katherine?"

Not the question she'd expected, but Amelia rolled with it.

"Of course I do. She's a little weird, but you can tell when you talk to her her heart is in the right place. Why?"

Meg took another deep breath.

"There are some girls at school that hassle her. They make fun of the stuff she likes and call her names behind her back. Real childish and cowardly, in my opinion," Meg spat.

"Yeah?" Amelia thought for a minute. Was Meg being punished for being Katherine's friend? The mama bear claws were starting to come out.

"Well, Katherine asked me if I thought she was scary like these girls are saying." Meg shook her head. "I told her I didn't think she was scary at all. I told her I liked her because she was different."

"That sounds like the right answer," Amelia replied softly.

"I thought so too," Meg answered firmly.

"But...it sounds like there is more to this. Are these girls turning on you because you are Katherine's friend?"

This was what Amelia was afraid of. The constantly looming threat of bullying had finally come. And bullying would lead to low self-esteem, falling grades, an eating disorder, drug abuse, suicide. In her mind, Amelia was already planning what she was going to say when she scheduled a meeting with the principal to make these girls stop or else.

"Mom, I couldn't care less what these girls think of me. I never liked them before. I don't like them now."

Stupefied, Amelia let out the breath she hadn't known she was holding. "So what is the problem?"

"Is there something wrong with me because I only have one friend?"

Amelia laughed. "No. My gosh. If you have one friend as good as Katherine, you are blessed. No, honey, there is nothing wrong with you for having just one friend." Amelia walked up to Meg and wrapped her arms around her. "In fact, I'm glad you picked a person so unique. That shows you don't care what the crowd thinks. I never pegged you for a follower, Meg. This just proves it, right?"

Meg smiled. That smile was going to win the heart of more than one boy in a few more short years, Amelia thought. Already, her daughter was almost as tall as her. Meg's body was changing in ways only a mother would notice.

Flashing back to when she was just a round little bundle of cuteness in a pink blanket, Amelia felt those tears trying to surface again. She shook her head.

"Is that all? Or is there more?"

"No." Meg smiled some more as she shook her head. "That's it."

"You sure? No worries about the current state of the economy? Concerns about asteroids heading toward Earth? I know I'm certainly apprehensive about the great UFO cover-ups."

"You are so weird." Meg laughed as she helped get the table set.

"Yeah, but you like weird. You just said so," Amelia said teasingly.

The two continued to bustle about the kitchen. Within minutes, the smell of bacon sizzling and pancakes on the griddle brought Adam up from the basement.

As they sat around the dinner table, the conversation jumped from school, to movies, to work, and finally landed, oddly enough, on the topic of Lila Bergman.

"She'll be working at the Gary-Fest, right, Mom?" Adam asked enthusiastically.

"Of course. My gosh, I'd be lost without her. She's as much a part of The Pink Cupcake as its hot-pink color. Can't have one without the other."

"Good," both kids said at the same time.

"Why do you ask?" Amelia squinted at her children, who eyed each other then looked innocently at their mother.

"No reason, really," Adam replied. "We just like her. She has funny stories."

"She does?" Amelia prodded. She knew they were right. Lila Bergman had a way of spinning a yarn that could keep you riveted.

She was a colorful personality, to say the least.

"She told me about when she was a teenager, she'd spend an afternoon with one boy, sneak in through the kitchen back door, quickly change into a new outfit, and come sauntering to the front door to go out with another boy at night." Meg giggled.

Amelia let out a burst of laughter then quickly composed herself.

"She told me that her brother took out their dad's car on a Friday and didn't have it back in the garage until Monday morning, just in time for their father to go to work, and when he opened the door, a hundred beer cans fell out," Adam added.

Both of Amelia's children were laughing hysterically. Unfortunately, it was contagious. Amelia laughed herself.

"I'm going to have to have a talk with that woman." She shook her head. "What kind of an influence is she?"

Both kids continued to laugh as they repeated more of Lila's stories. It was music to Amelia's ears.

Chapter Three

Lila looked at Amelia with the most angelic face, folding her hands neatly in front of her.

"I don't know what stories you're talking about," she muttered, nearly choking on the laughter she was trying to hold back.

"Lila Bergman, don't play innocent with me," Amelia said scoldingly with her own bursts of laughter tripping up her words. "Here, stir this batter."

"Do you mean to tell me you never entertained your children with stories about crazy things you did as a teenager?" Lila took up her station at the mixer and helped prepare the batter for the day's special, which was chocolate cherry truffle.

"I didn't do anything worth bragging about. Plus, anything I did do that might have been the slightest bit scandalous, I certainly don't want them to know about." She chuckled, shaking her head.

"Well"–Lila pushed her bright-red hair back from her face with the palm of her hand–"truthfully, I think you should take a hide to both of them for laughing at me. You have no idea how difficult it was to keep my social life afloat. It was quite draining."

Lila stopped the blender as she had been taught, removed the bowl, and finished stirring with a plastic spoon.

"Do you realize how many toads I had to kiss before I found a prince? Some of them I had to kiss more than once just to be sure."

Amelia's eyes were watering as she laughed.

"I'm sorry if you find my past so... indecent." Lila looked at Amelia and batted her long, false eyelashes then tugged the top of her shirt close at the collar.

"It's your indecency that makes you so alluring." Amelia broke loose laughing.

Not only did Lila crack up as well, but several of the owners of the neighboring trucks were peeking in the direction of The Pink Cupcake, trying to see who was having so much fun so early in the morning.

"Hey!" came a male voice from the side of the Philly Cheese Steak truck. "Keep it down in there! Some of us are trying to work!"

Amelia and Lila instantly fell silent like two schoolgirls and looked out from the order window to see the very handsome salt-and-pepper-haired man who owned the Philly Cheese Steak truck smiling up at them, his blue eyes twinkling.

"Are you talking to us?" Lila barked over Amelia's shoulder.

"I am." He took a sip from the Styrofoam cup he was holding. "What kind of people have that much fun at this hour?"

Amelia, blushing, just shook her head. She tried to ignore Lila, who was jabbing her in the back with the clean end of her spoon.

"I'm Amelia," she said, leaning out the window and extending her hand. "This is Lila." She jerked her thumb, pointing behind her. Lila smiled and waved, still tapping Amelia in the back.

"Name's Gavin." He reached up and shook Amelia's hand. She could feel the muscles in his wrist and calluses on his palm. "Took you long enough."

"What are you talking about?"

"Well, I've just been trying to get your attention since you moved in next door to me."

"Is that so?" Amelia withdrew her hand and watched Gavin's face. He was looking at her intently. "Well, a girl like me is busy with the business and kids and..."

"Husband?"

Amelia tilted her head to the left and clicked her tongue.

"Subtle." She smirked. "No. I'm divorced."

"Oh." Gavin smiled broadly. "Well, Amelia. It was very nice meeting you." He peeked behind her. "You too, Lila." His eyes met Amelia's. "I hope you don't mind if I stop by to borrow a cup of sugar some time."

"She's got more than enough to share," Lila piped up, bumping Amelia with her hip.

Gavin chuckled and gave Amelia a quick wave before heading back to his own truck, looking over his shoulder once more before he disappeared inside the vehicle.

Once he was safely out of earshot, Lila began her questioning.

"What do you mean you're not interested?" Lila asked. "No one says you've got to marry him, but maybe go catch a movie or grab something to eat that isn't cupcakes or Philly cheese steaks."

"I know, but I've seen that kind of guy before. He's probably used those same lines on half the ladies in half the food trucks just on this block alone. Besides, I can find myself a date if I wanted one."

"Yes." Lila nodded. "There is a certain detective I've noticed can't seem to go an entire week without stopping by to buy cupcakes for the entire police station."

"Dan is just a friend." Amelia felt as if her antiperspirant had given out.

"It isn't written anywhere that you can't have more than one friend."

"Yeah, Mr. Philly Cheese Steak probably has lots of *friends*." Amelia used her fingers to quote the word friends.

"I don't know," Lila insisted. "I've been keeping an eye on him, and well, he doesn't seem to flirt with many people. In fact, once the grill is sizzling, he's pretty focused."

"What is your interest in all this?" Amelia asked.

Lila stopped what she was doing and looked at Amelia lovingly.

"When my ex-husband left me, I felt very alone. But not as alone as I felt when he was around."

Amelia frowned and gave Lila a puzzled but sympathetic look.

"He had said he loved everything about me." Lila took a deep breath. "Until he realized they were things he lacked in himself. Then my strengths became weaknesses, my theme song became just uncoordinated, messy noise. I became an embarrassment to him."

She shook her head and studied her bright-red nails.

"You? An embarrassment? You're the life of the party, Lila."

Chuckling, Lila smiled.

"To *you* I am. To Jacob, I was a roommate, not a wife, who was ignorant about everything and shamed by nothing." Amelia watched as Lila's eyes seemed to harden into icy-blue diamonds. "According to him, I should have worn a bag over my head to hide my face from the world. How could I stand for people to know my beliefs, my lineage, my utter stupidity?"

Swallowing hard, Amelia remembered her own feelings of inadequacy, of failure when her ex-husband had begun his campaign to criticize her every move.

"Surprisingly, when he told me he was leaving me for another woman, I felt relief. Sure, I had a grieving period, thinking I should have changed my ways or had the reconstructive surgery or gone back to school. A million things I should have done differently so he'd have loved me more."

Amelia held her breath. Did she hear Lila right? Reconstructive surgery?

"After he left, I stayed close to home, didn't return calls, and rarely spoke when I went out anywhere. But then I thought better of it. There was nothing I could have done that would have made Jacob change."

"Lila, did you say reconstructive surgery?" Amelia gulped.

As if a light had suddenly been shone in her eyes, Lila blinked, shook her head, and waved her hand in front of her face, as if those two words, "reconstructive surgery," meant nothing.

"My point is that friends surface in unlikely places. And sometimes we have to force ourselves to smile first in order to find them."

It was obvious Lila had slipped. And in her typical carefree style, she waved it away like a pesky gnat. Amelia silently agreed to let her off the hook...this time.

"Did Jacob ever apologize to you?" she asked.

"Not in words. But, like most men who realize when they have made a mistake, he opened his wallet." Lila winked. "The first thing I did when I decided to start living again was I ditched the jet-black hair for red. He hated redheads."

"You had black hair?" Amelia squinted. "I just can't see it. You look like...*you* with red hair. I like your choice."

Lila smiled.

"The next thing I did was send letters—yes, letters not emails, but elegant, hand-written letters to all the people who had known Jacob and I together. I just sent them letters to say hello and hoping they were well. Out of thirty-five letters, I received thirty-two responses, all kind and loving and funny. I had many more friends than I had thought. A few of them were quite handsome and quite single."

"Did you ever speak to Jacob again?"

Lila shook her head.

"No. He's with his mistress in Australia, probably doing to her what he did to me." She shook her head sadly.

"Do you miss him?"

"I miss the him I knew when we were younger. But not that much. Just because I've become comfortable with myself doesn't mean I don't still wish an army of fire ants wouldn't find his groin area."

Amelia knew that feeling all too well. She looked at Lila closely, knowing her friend had gone to the doctor's several weeks ago. Those two words, reconstructive surgery, echoed behind her conscious thoughts. Just as she was about to ask, Lila spoke again.

"What I'm trying to say in my own long-winded kind of way is that life is a banquet and most people are starving."

Amelia laughed.

"I can't take credit for that line. It's from *Auntie Mame*. Rosalind Russell had it right. In that movie, her billionaire husband fell off the side of a mountain. If only we could all be so lucky."

Both of them laughed.

"You are my hero, Lila." Amelia sighed, touching her friend's hand. "I won't say I'll go out with Mr. Philly Cheese Steak today. But I'll consider it. I'm just not as bold as you are."

Lila nodded and smiled. "No, perhaps not. But you did make that radical change to your hair, cutting off about eight inches a few months ago." Lila smirked. "Isn't it funny how change starts so small?"

Without thinking, Amelia lifted her hand to her shorn neck. She had just gotten a trim and loved the low maintenance of her hairstyle. But her thoughts went to her own ex-husband. If only John would move to an entirely different continent. Not that that would ease the feeling of anger and rejection she still felt over his infidelity, but it would be comforting to know she'd never have to see him again.

As it was, both Adam and Meg wanted their father to stop by the Gary Food Fest to check out the festivities and show his support. Amelia, on the other hand, knew the critical, judgmental jerk that was John O'Malley would find all kinds of reasons to roll his eyes or shrug at her accomplishments. Their last conversation on the phone had been quick but loaded with unvoiced anger.

"Jennifer and I want to pick up the kids early. Can you have them ready?"

"Sure, John. How early is early?"

"Well, Jennifer asked if Friday right after school was okay. She's leaving for a visit to her parents' house early Saturday morning and wanted to see the kids before she left."

Amelia felt her gut twisting with jealousy she never knew she had. Why was this *girl* her ex-husband was dating taking such an interest in *her* children? Was this normal?

"No problem, John. That's fine. I know the kids will be fine with that. They are also expecting you to be at the food fest in two weeks. You'll take them, right?"

"I'll be there for sure. Jennifer doesn't like all that fried stuff, and you know we are both trying to watch what we eat."

Amelia rolled her eyes just as Meg came down the steps.

"Are you talking to Dad?" she asked with wide eyes. Amelia nodded, and before she could stop her she snagged the phone from her mother's hand.

"You better make it to the food fest, Dad. Mom's truck is one of the most popular ones out there."

Amelia could hear John laugh in his condescending way but said nothing.

After a few giggles and a nod, Meg handed the phone back to her mother.

"Okay, so, you're all good, John. We'll see you."

Without another word, the phone went dead, and Amelia shook her head. Why did he have to make it so hard? Why couldn't he just be a normal person?

It was because of John that the idea of going out with Mr. Philly Cheese Steak—Gavin—was so scary. Sure, he was really handsome and charming and quick with the double meanings in his words. Yup, he had all the trappings of a brute in disguise.

She didn't need all that fluff. To be honest, she didn't know what she wanted.

Snapping her out of her thoughts was the sound of wind chimes coming from her pocket. She pulled out her phone and looked at the number.

It was Detective Dan Walishovsky from the Gary Police Department calling with his weekly order of cupcakes for the station and to chitchat for a few minutes. Amelia couldn't help but smile. The negative thoughts about her ex-husband quickly melted away as she answered the phone.

After spending time with the detective on a real stakeout, Amelia had found that the detective, Dan, was not only interesting, but very funny, although a smile for him consisted of his lips bending only slightly at the corners.

"Hi," she answered happily, breaking out into a wide smile.

Chapter Four

"I can't believe how many people are here already," Meg exclaimed as she and her best friend, Katherine, leaned out the serving window of The Pink Cupcake truck. "I thought we'd be the only ones out of school early."

Gary Food Fest took place from Friday at three o'clock thru Sunday at nine o'clock in the evening. The trucks were locked up tight from about midnight until six in the morning each day.

"Why don't you guys go check out the competition for us?" Amelia suggested. "Lila and I have to get baking, so we won't need you until the customers start showing up."

Meg and Katherine nodded with excitement and hopped off the truck. Amelia had gotten permission to pull Meg and Katherine out of school an hour early to help. She thought working would be at least as valuable as learning what the main export of Guam was in her last period of social studies.

"Be back in about an hour," Amelia called. "And don't eat from any of the other bakery trucks!"

"Okay, Mom!" Meg called over her shoulder.

It wasn't long before the truck was filled with the sweet smell of cake. The night before, Amelia and Lila had put in some overtime. Together, they had made several dozen of the peanut butter and jelly cupcakes that had become an instant favorite plus their staple, chocolate truffle raspberry cupcakes. But, on the truck, they were now baking apple crumble cupcakes that were loaded with finely chopped apples, tons of cinnamon, and a hint of caramel.

The inside became very hot very quickly as all three ovens were baking at the same time and would be for at least half the day.

Grabbing two ice waters from their cooler, Amelia looked to Lila.

"I'll buy you a cold one," she joked.

Lila nodded, grabbed the bottle, and ran the cool condensation over her forehead as they climbed off the back of the truck.

Surveying the area, they saw many of their usual neighbors were not in their usual spots. Instead of the Philly Cheese Steak truck to their left, there was a gyro truck called Pegasus. To their right was a truck boasting Chicago-style pizza. Next to them was the Tofu Express.

"Who in their right mind would pay to eat tofu out of a truck?" Lila puzzled.

"Now, come on, Lila. We don't like to criticize other food trucks, do we?"

Lila looked at Amelia as if she suddenly smelled something bad.

"Have you ever tasted tofu?"

"It's bean curd, right?"

Lila shivered. "Just the sound of that makes me lose my appetite. They should be chased out of here with clubs and torches."

Amelia laughed.

Next to Tofu Express was a tiny cart attached to a bicycle. The words Hot Dogs, Polish Sausages, Brats were painted on the sides of the white box at the front of the bike. Attached to the seat was a large American flag.

"I wonder if that guy paid the whole fee for that spot just to have his little hot dog cart there," Amelia mused, feeling pity for the man. He looked wild, with long hair in a ponytail, cut-off jean shorts, and red Converse high-top gym shoes.

"He's an entrepreneur. In its rawest form." Lila smiled and waved to the man, who seemed to be mumbling to himself as he gave her a quick salute.

It wasn't long before the grounds were filled with people. Included with the Gary Food Fest was a carnival just off the pond where Amelia had wanted to anchor The Pink Cupcake for the weekend but couldn't afford.

"We've still got a good spot, don't you think?" she asked Lila, who was sprinkling the final topping of cinnamon-caramel crunch over the tops of the latest batch of cupcakes. "I mean we're actually just off the main drag. It isn't like we are in a corner or anything."

"This is perfect for us. We are in the shade, and they didn't move the picnic tables. People will be drawn this way to take a load off."

The distinct sound of the carnival attractions was now a steady thump-thump-thump in the background as heavy metal music blared from rides called The Barn Burner or The Octopus. Screams of wild teenagers and young couples could be heard as they left their stomachs behind on wildly unstable-looking contraptions that dropped from two hundred feet in the air only to slowly climb back up to their perch and plummet again.

"I'm just not sure it was smart to have the food fest with those kinds of carnival rides. You know some kid is going to insist on a couple cupcakes plus slices of pizza, washing it all down with a root beer and then begging his parents to take him on The Whizzer or whatever. All that stuff will come right back up," Lila stated with her hand on her hip.

"Eww!" Amelia chuckled. "You painted a very vivid picture just then. Thanks."

Just then, Meg and Katherine came carefully into the back of the truck. Amelia took one look at them and stopped what she was doing.

"Meg?" She saw her daughter was as pale as a ghost. "Honey, what's the matter?"

Meg's eyes filled with tears.

Amelia looked to Katherine and squared her shoulders.

"What happened?" she demanded.

"That guy over there." Katherine pointed to the man with the simple hot dog cart on his bicycle. "He called Meg over and said something to her."

Looking at her daughter, Amelia didn't see the little girl who loved old movies and still slept with a little stuffed white snowman that wore a green hat. She saw a young woman who was getting curves in all the places she was supposed to and who unknowingly displayed her innocence. The mama bear claws were coming out again, and Amelia gently took her daughter's hands. Lila quickly grabbed a bottle of ice water that she handed the girl.

"Meg, what did he say to you?" Amelia asked as gently as she could.

Meg shook her head. She looked at Katherine for some assistance, but all she got was a shrug.

"He just called her, you know, hey, hey, and waved her over. The guy is driving a hot dog cart on wheels, and it isn't like we weren't in full view of everyone. She didn't do anything wrong, Ms. Harley."

"Oh, no," Amelia said soothingly. "I didn't think that for a second." She looked out the window and saw the man serving a tall, lanky teenager a hot dog. It looked as if he was mumbling to himself the whole while. "Look, your brother should be here. He can walk you guys home and..."

"No, Mom," Meg whined. "It wasn't anything. He just caught me off guard, you know? He just said something about my legs."

Amelia looked at Lila.

"Your legs?"

Meg shook her head and wiped her tears away. She was coming back from the shock, and anger was starting to set in.

"Yeah, you know, how good they look and stuff." Her cheeks blazed red. Meg was not the kind of girl who sought the attention of the boys, at least not yet. Amelia was sure her daughter hadn't expected it to feel so uncomfortable.

Taking a deep breath, Amelia nodded.

"I hate to tell you this, but you girls are going to experience this a few times in life. There are still plenty of good gentlemen in the world who will compliment you properly. But there will always be hot-dog vendors, too."

The comment made Meg and Katherine laugh.

"Do me a favor. If you want to stay and hand out samples, stay in front of the truck and away from that end. If that guy comes anywhere near the truck, you both get inside, got it?"

Both girls nodded and smiled.

"Hey, I brought you both a present." Lila quickly grabbed their attention with the word *present*. She reached over to the cubby that held her purse and pulled out two hot-pink aprons.

"Wow!" Both girls were thrilled. "They totally match the truck!"

Slipping them on, both girls fussed over each other tying the long strings in the back and thrusting their hands into the deep pockets.

"Here." Amelia handed each of them a plastic tray with hot-pink paper cupcake cups filled with crumbled cupcakes. "Give these out. One sample per person. Stay away from the weirdo."

Both girls nodded and then stepped off the truck. "I'll bet he washes his feet in that box," Katherine muttered, making Meg laugh.

"Yeah, or he has the head of his mother who died six years ago in there," Meg added.

"Right next to the brats!" Katherine answered, causing both girls to roar with laughter.

"Oh, it is on," Amelia hissed at Lila. "I'm going to go over there and make sure that guy doesn't even think of looking in this direction."

"Want my mace?" Lila offered.

"Nope. Got my bare hands this time."

Making sure Meg and Katherine were not looking, Amelia stepped off the truck. But she hadn't made it two feet before a mob of reporters, security guards, and other gawkers got in her way.

"Mr. Mayor! Mr. Mayor!" came shouts from the reporters, who held small recorders, pulling along men with cameras on their shoulders as security guards shielded the portly man in the middle of the whirlwind from actually coming in contact with the commoners.

"What the...?" Amelia wasn't sure whom she wanted to go after first. The jerk that had accosted her daughter, or the jerk that had jacked up the price of her space. It was a real toss-up.

Mayor Richard M. Pearl had been the mayor of Gary for almost two decades. Years of supposed pay-to-play schemes and the buying and selling of city jobs had not only lined his pockets, but filled every empty seat in city hall with a friend of a friend or relative of the Pearl family. He was in a snug little bubble where no one could touch him and no one dared try. The man had a full head of wavy black hair that was going gray. His nose and cheeks were always red, and Amelia doubted he had seen his toes from beneath his ample gut since he started his life in politics. A man like him always ate well when someone else footed the bill.

Amelia remembered a few years back during a particularly aggressive campaign season that an underdog, a virtual nobody, was slowly climbing in the polls by shining a light on half a dozen scandals Mayor Pearl was directly involved in.

The guy's name was Porter or Parker. Amelia couldn't quite remember. But she did remember when the news came in that Porter or Parker had committed suicide by throwing himself in front of a train just one week before the election.

"The pressure got to him," John had said to Amelia. He was an avid Pearl supporter. "The guy wasn't cut out for politics. He just knew how to smear. They probably had something on him that was too much, so he killed himself."

"But the stuff he said was true," Amelia remembered stating meekly to John. "Most of the proof was the mayor's own words." She shrugged.

"Amelia, no one knows less about politics than you," John snapped and stormed out of the room. From that day on, Amelia had always found the opposing party much more appealing than the one John staked so much faith in. If that weren't enough to hate Mayor Pearl, then the process she'd had to go through to get her food truck license certainly was.

Pulling up her courage from the bottom of her shoes, Amelia decided she might just ask the mayor why her spot cost so much more for this weekend when she lived in the town and was there every day already. Why didn't he charge the "out-of-towners" more? Tofu Express indeed.

Just as she started to march up to Mayor Pearl, she was quickly pushed back by reporters and security.

"Mr. Mayor!" The shout came from a man. "Mr. Mayor! How about lunch on me?" It was the long-haired freak with the hot-dog bike. "Best hot dogs in three states!"

With the offer of a free meal, the mayor stopped and turned around. Smiling and thrusting his chest out to the cameras, he began to speak.

"This is it. See. This is what it's all about. See." He jerked his thumb toward the man, who was holding out two hot dogs cupped in silver tin foil so they'd stay warm. "See. We encourage the small businessman. That's what this is all about." He nodded to a particularly large guard wearing a bullet-proof vest beneath his windbreaker. The guy had pudgy cheeks and blond hair he combed over his head and wore mirrored sunglasses. The guard turned, pushed his way to the vendor, and took the hot dogs from him. Slowly, he pushed his way back through the crowd as the mayor spoke to the cameras.

"Mr. Mayor. Do you have a minute to talk?" the vendor called. The other body-guards set themselves in between Pearl and anyone else looking to get close to him.

"It's a great event. See. These are great people." The mayor took the hot dogs and peeled the foil back away from his gaping maw. "We've got over three thousand food trucks from all over the state here this weekend. There is a carnival just across the pond. No one does it like Gary. See. Everyone should come down and sample some of this great food." He opened wide and shoveled in almost the entire hot dog in one bite.

"Mr. Mayor. George Pilsen was my brother!"

"Pilsen!" Amelia muttered, snapping her fingers. That was the guy who they said killed himself jumping in front of a train. Wait. What did that man just say? With the crowd, the carnival, and the cooking food,

Amelia was sure she could have heard a pin drop.

Chapter Five

"Mr. Mayor! What do you have to say to his family? His wife and three children who've had to grow up without him?"

Pearl whispered to his henchmen, and they bolted into action.

"I'd encourage everyone to come on down. See. We'd love to have you." He smiled and chuckled for the camera. It was obvious the hippy hot-dog vendor had caught old Mayor Pearl off guard. Amelia stood back and grinned at his discomfort even as the entourage jostled her out of the way.

She looked toward The Pink Cupcake. Lila had brought the girls inside, and they were all looking out the serving window with interest.

"It's been three years, Mr. Mayor!" the man continued to call out. "Three years, and you have yet to offer any condolences! You have yet to answer about the airport land grab! My brother knew what you were doing, Mr. Mayor!"

The man quickly hurried back to his bike.

"You killed my brother, Mayor Pearl! How many other people have you killed? Where is Susan Connor?"

Amelia's eyes widened. This was better than television. Susan Connor was the supposed mistress of Mayor Pearl who had gone missing without a trace.

"My brother knew where she was. She was going to talk before you killed him!"

The bodyguards were not moving fast enough.

"Shut him up!" the mayor hissed to his closest confidant. He threw the other hot dog on the ground, and before anyone could criticize him for littering, he was shuffling away, with the entire group of reporters fawning all over the man as usual.

Sure, they couldn't interview every crazy with a complaint against the mayor. But this? This was different. Obviously, the hippy that scared Meg was touched in the head. Whether it was from grief or mental illness or a little of both, Amelia felt relief that she had never made it up to him to say anything.

She watched as he pedaled away as if the devil were chasing him before the mayor's bodyguards could get to him.

"Wow!" Amelia turned to the truck. "That was better than television."

"See, I told you that guy was just a loon." Katherine elbowed Meg, who nodded. "He's gone now, so we can breathe easy."

"I'll bet he didn't even pay a fee like my mom did to have that cart here," Meg stated, folding her arms in front of her.

"Still, stay close to the truck, girls," Amelia instructed them as she ushered them off and took her place at the window with Lila.

"Now that was worth it. If you would have gotten that fancy property by the pond, we'd have never gotten this ringside seat." Lila took a sip of water. "Couldn't have happened to a better guy."

Before they could enjoy a long discussion on their mutual distrust of Mayor Pearl and wonder what the press would actually report on the confrontation, they were slammed with a wave of customers that seemed to have no end. The girls gave out all their samples, resulting in so many sales, Amelia lost count after thirty.

"Hey, Spaz." Amelia heard her son's voice as he greeted his sister.

"Nerd," Meg replied. "Hi, Amy."

"Hi, Meg." Amy's voice was soft and in complete contrast to her purple hair. "I love your aprons."

The kids chitchatted for a moment as Meg and Katherine, at speeds topping one hundred miles an hour, retold the story of the hot dog vendor, the mayor, and the big show Amy and Adam had missed.

"I guess it turned out good you had your regular spot, Mom," Adam said as he and Amy climbed up the back steps into the truck. "Boy, it's hot in here." He wiped his head.

"Is there anything we can do to help, Ms. Harley?" Amy offered.

"Yes." Lila rattled off a list of supplies they were running dangerously low on. "Take my car and go pick these things up."

"Lila, you've been working all morning, and I don't even think you've stepped off this truck once. Why don't you go? Get some fresh air and..."

"And leave you here with these rookies? No offense, kids, but you just don't have the stuff like I do." She gave Adam a wink. "You have your license, right?"

Adam nodded enthusiastically.

Looking at Amelia, Lila raised her eyebrows.

"Please, Mom?"

"You better be extra careful."

He smiled broadly and looked at Amy.

"Here is the list. Now, my car is parked just down the street in front of my apartment building with the doorman."

"What color is it?" Adam asked, gently taking the keys from her hand.

"It's a red Mercedes with Lila on the license plate."

Both Adam and Amy's eyes popped.

"Be careful, and pick up these things for your mom then come right back. No shenanigans."

"Don't worry, Lila. We're not Irish." Adam smiled. Before Amelia could protest, he had the keys and the list in his pocket and Amy's hand in his.

"Are you crazy?" Amelia shook her head. "Letting him drive the Mercedes?"

"What? I'm insured."

"I'm glad you see it as that simple." Amelia looked again to see her son walking away down the street where Lila lived.

"What are you going to do when that boy goes off to college?" Lila said teasingly.

"Before or after my nervous breakdown?"

Both ladies chuckled and finished up the last of the supplies for a quick batch of double chocolate truffle raspberry cupcakes. The minutes ticked by as Amelia nervously watched her watch.

Ten minutes. Twenty minutes. Half an hour. Forty-five minutes.

"That boy is going to get a beating so severe. If he wasn't in an accident, he'll believe he was, he'll be so black and blue," Amelia fumed. She really only said these things to hide her fear that he had gotten hurt or perhaps damaged Lila's car and was afraid to come back.

Just then, he came up the back of the truck. He and Amy looked as if they were in shock.

"Where have you been?" Amelia immediately said scoldingly. "What took you so long? I've been worried to death."

"Mom, it wasn't our fault. We couldn't get back in."

"What are you talking about?" Amelia snapped. "You park the car where you found it, and you walk across the..." She stopped as she saw dozens of police descending on the park. "What's going on?"

"That's what I'm trying to tell you. All the streets are blocked. Didn't you hear all the sirens?"

Amelia thought that she might have heard something like sirens, but they had been so busy and she was so focused on waiting for Adam to come back with Lila's luxury car that she might have been a little distracted.

"There are fire trucks and paramedics all over down State Street. They had roadblocks up. People were running all over the place, and police were pushing back reporters and gawkers," Amy replied. "At first we thought maybe something had blown up, but we didn't hear anything that sounded like an explosion. Then we thought maybe a riot or something, but there wasn't any screaming or anything like that. The cops weren't rushing around, and none of them were in riot gear. We couldn't tell what was happening. It just looked like they pulled out every emergency vehicle in the entire city of Gary to tackle whatever had gone on."

"We almost laughed when we heard what all the fuss was about." Adam nodded to Amy. "I don't think the Kennedy assassination had as big a turnout of emergency vehicles."

"They said Mayor Pearl was being rushed to the hospital," Amy added. "They wouldn't let us through. And they looked through all your groceries and stuff." She offered up the torn paper bag she was trying to hold together.

"Oh, honey, here. Let me." Lila took the bag, and Amelia took the other from her son.

"From what we could hear, he had some kind of episode or something." Adam shrugged.

Both Amelia and Lila looked at each other.

"They wouldn't have a bunch of cops combing the place if it was just food poisoning," Amelia mused. She looked out the back door, and as if he had heard her thoughts, Detective Dan Walishovsky was making his way toward The Pink Cupcake.

Turning to Adam and Amy, Amelia gave them both a hug.

"You guys had me worried." She looked lovingly at her son. "Did you like driving Lila's car?"

"It was a little too nerve-wracking to enjoy. I like our sedan better," he whispered.

"You keep up that kind of thinking, and you're going to have a very happy life. Okay, glad you kids are safe. How about taking some pictures for me, and you can have the rest of the night off...with pay."

"Really?" Adam smiled.

"We did a lot better than I thought we would. We are in the black for the next twenty-four hours." She looked at Lila and gave her a wink. "But take your sister with you. And keep an eye on her."

"No problem, Mom. Thanks." He and Amy slipped down the steps, and Amelia could hear them greeting Dan as they passed by.

"Of all the places to stop first, he picks here. Hmmm...how convenient," Lila said teasingly as she set to cleaning things up.

The police were like a blue wave guiding people toward the opposite end of the park and roping off half the area where Chicago Style Pizza, Pegasus Gyros, Tofu Express, The Pink Cupcake, plus a couple dozen more trucks were all corralled.

"Dan?" Amelia's voice was low and shaky. "What is going on? Please don't tell me."

"Hi, Amelia. Lila." He nodded toward both women. "I hate to do this to you, but this whole area has got to be cornered off."

"What? For how long?"

"Tonight. Maybe tomorrow."

"But what for?"

"The mayor. He's sick. They think it came from one of the trucks this way."

"You're closing us up for food poisoning? Do you know how many guys are going to be on their pots all night from eating bacon-wrapped scallops out of a truck from the Aquarius Diner over on the eastern end of the park?" Lila protested. "No one is closing them down."

Dan looked at Lila with what was as much of a smile as he could muster. That was a slight curve at the right corner of his mouth. But when he looked at Amelia, his heart broke.

"Dan, we had a record-setting afternoon." Amelia shook her head, her eyes wide. "This isn't even the peak. That comes tomorrow."

"Believe me, if it were just for food poisoning, I'd have no problem directing my boys around your truck. But we have reason to believe it's more than that."

Both Amelia and Lila looked at each other.

"When I say he's been poisoned, I mean they are rushing him to County right now. I'm afraid it isn't just bacon-wrapped scallops."

"He didn't eat here, Dan." Lila's voice was calm.

"No. In fact..." Amelia's eyes bugged. "He ate a hot dog. I saw him. And then there was that whole kerfuffle."

"What kerfuffle?" Dan pulled out his notebook from the inside of his jacket. He always looked as if he'd stepped out of an old episode of Dragnet. His tall frame was perfect for a droopy suit. He wore hard shoes that had to be a size thirteen if they were an inch. Although he wasn't wrinkled or disheveled, Amelia always got the impression that he was working very hard when she saw him. His clothes were as serious as the job.

Standing closer to Dan, Amelia retold the story about the man with the hot dog cart. She told him everything, starting with Meg's encounter all the way up to his exchange with the mayor. Amelia might have been wrong, but she thought Dan had become more ruffled by what the suspect had said to Meg than his possibly poisoning the mayor.

"Can you describe this guy for me?"

Both Amelia and Lila gave a detailed description of the fellow. They had gotten a very good look at his face. But the fact that he'd claimed to be the late politician George Pilsen's brother would make tracking him down much easier.

"Dan, do you really think you need to close us up for the rest of the weekend?" Amelia pleaded.

"I'll tell my guys to start here. They've got to comb the grounds." He rubbed the back of his neck. "I'm not going to lie to you, Amelia. If they find anything on the grounds, they'll have to close off this area. And the truck needs to stay put."

Had it been anyone else, Amelia would have used every obscenity she knew, of which she was sure there were three, and threatened they try and stop her from operating her business. But it was Dan. He was just doing his job, and she knew that if there were any other way, he'd take it.

"I'll drive you home, Amelia," Lila offered, putting her hand on her friend's shoulder. "Let's just get ready as if everything is going to go off without a hitch tomorrow."

"Lila is right," Dan said encouragingly.

Amelia looked up at him and felt the tingling of tears trying to surface in her eyes. Shaking her head, she gave him a weak smile. He was a gentleman and asked a few beat cops to help carry the supplies Adam had bought to Lila's car. Lila led the way, but Dan took Amelia by the arm and held her back for a moment.

"I will do everything I can do to get you up and running by tomorrow."

"I know you will, Dan." She smiled up at him.

"I think you should know that according to the Gary Food Fest, there were no hot dog vendors listed."

Amelia blinked.

"This brother of George Pilsen didn't have a permit to be here."

"Hmm, Meg and Katherine both said that about that guy. How do you know?"

"Well, when you said you were going to participate in the event, I took it upon myself to see what the competition looked like." He knitted his eyebrows. "I got a list of all the vendors. Not a hot dog vendor among the group. I guess the old American staple isn't as glamorous as deep-fried pickles on a stick."

Amelia chuckled.

"I'm touched you'd check and see who our baking rivals might be."

Dan's right eyebrow shot up. Amelia would never say it out loud, but she thought he looked devastatingly handsome when he did that. She blushed and quickly looked at the floor.

"I'll walk you to Lila's car."

"No. That's okay." She would have loved the escort, but her mind began counting numbers in her head. "Please, work with your team and let me know as soon as you can if we can come back tomorrow. Even if you have to call at two in the morning."

Dan nodded, and they exited the truck together. Without a second of hesitation, Dan took to shouting orders to the detectives and uniformed officers, to which they eagerly responded. Detective Walishovsky was a respected man among the ranks at Gary PD. He was known for being tough, fair, honest, and not to be messed with.

Letting out a sigh, Amelia made her way to Lila's Mercedes. She thanked the officers for their help and climbed in, and both women headed to Amelia's house. The kids were already there and were told about the truck being under quarantine. But the excitement of another mystery seemed to outweigh their disappointment.

Chapter Six

"If you are just joining us this morning, breaking news. Mayor Richard M. Pearl has died. He was pronounced dead at County Medical Hospital yesterday evening after collapsing at the Gary Food Fest. Foul play has not been ruled out. Pearl had held public office for twenty-four years as mayor of the city of Gary, nearly making his silver anniversary. Services are being held at the..."

Amelia shut the TV off, shaking her head.

"They didn't say anything about the weird guy yelling at him yesterday." Meg pointed to the black television while taking a bite out of an apple.

"That makes me wonder." Amelia thought it strange. In this day and age, there had to be dozens of versions of that incident. There were at least that many people watching, and Amelia knew she saw a few of them recording with their phones. Not to mention the reporters that were right there.

"Wonder what, Mom?" Adam asked before intentionally bumping into his sister, who elbowed him back.

"Nothing." She pursed her lips. Looking at her watch, she let out a sigh. She turned toward the window and saw a beautifully gray day with a cool breeze rustling the trees. It was a perfect day, in her opinion. It was a perfect day to be in her truck, baking. Instead, she found herself pacing the floor.

Dan hadn't called in the middle of the night to let her know she could get back to the truck and fire up the ovens. She was tempted to call him and ask for an update, but she knew he was already doing her a favor by keeping her in the loop. If he didn't call, it was because he didn't have any news. Not yet, anyway.

"How did your pictures turn out? Were you able to get anything good?" Amelia asked, quickly changing the subject.

"Well, I didn't get any pictures. I mean I got off a few, but..."

"You didn't tell her?" Meg chirped.

"Tell me what?"

"No, Big Mouth." Adam nudged his sister. "I didn't want to bother you when you got home last night. You looked like you didn't need any more bad news."

Amelia folded her arms in front of her and sat on the arm of the couch, facing the kitchen.

"When Amy and I were bringing back the groceries, the cops stopped us, you know, to see where we were going. What we were up to. They took my camera and erased all the photos. There was a really good one of Amy and me on there, too."

"Did they say why?" Amelia looked sternly at her son.

"No. But I didn't ask any questions. I started to look for Dan. But by the time I saw him, it looked like he had his hands full. I didn't want to sound like a whiney kid." He looked at Meg when he said those words, to which she stuck her tongue out at him.

Amelia's eyebrows shot up to her forehead. None of this surprised her.

"Sorry, Mom."

"It's no big deal. I mean it's a big deal that someone erased your photos, but it's not a big deal to me that we don't have any. I'll ask Dan about that. See what he has to say." She stood up and put her hands on her hips. "In the meantime, you guys have a couple of chores each. Then, well, the rest of the day is yours, I guess."

"What are you going to do?" Meg asked, pushing herself up from the table.

"Sit around and wait for the phone to ring, I guess."

A loud knock on the door startled all of them.

"Who could that be at this hour on a Saturday?" Amelia grumbled and went to the front door.

"Good morning," Dan said, holding two large coffees in his hands.

"Good morning, Dan." Amelia blinked, her hand again going nervously to the back of her neck. "You're up early."

"You mean up late." He smirked as Amelia stepped aside, letting him come in.

"Hey, Detective!" Meg waved cheerfully as she bopped upstairs.

"Hi, Dan!" Adam called from the kitchen before retreating to his teenager cave in the basement.

"Meg. Adam," Dan replied, his voice deep.

"Let me guess," Amelia started as she closed the door behind him. "I'm closed for the event, right?"

"It doesn't look good. We still might be able to get everyone back in their trucks by tomorrow."

Amelia's shoulders slumped.

"It's better than nothing, I suppose. I'll never get the traffic at that time like I did yesterday." She looked at Dan as they made their way to the kitchen. "Please don't think I'm blaming you, because I'm not. But why the heck couldn't the mayor have dropped dead on the other side of the pond? And I don't mean England."

Dan shook his head, chuckling a little as he took a seat at the kitchen table.

"We're trying to track down that hot dog vendor. We think that guy is a lot more dangerous than he appeared."

Amelia's heart jumped to her throat as she thought of what he'd said to Meg.

"Why do you say that?"

"As it turns out, the mayor was poisoned. They won't know with what until the autopsy. I put my money on arsenic."

"Arsenic?" Amelia pulled the lid off her coffee and took a sip. "Sort of an old-fashioned method, wouldn't you say? Who poisons people with arsenic these days?"

Dan shrugged as he sipped his coffee.

"Actually, that is pretty genius," Amelia said, looking out her kitchen window. "You have a grudge against someone, there is a food festival going on, meet up with your nemesis and sprinkle a little arsenic on their samples, and it's like finding a needle in a haystack. There's no telling where the poison may have come from. Yikes, you really think that hot dog peddler was that crafty?"

"Maybe." Dan nodded. "You're right, too. According to witnesses, the mayor had consumed several samples in addition to the hot dog you and Lila saw him eat."

"That doesn't surprise me. If it didn't cost him, he'd have his hands in it. Mayor Pearl was a crook from where I'm sitting, and I'm just a nobody. My question is when you catch the guy who did it, do you prosecute or give him a medal?"

It was the first time Dan had ever burst out laughing, and it almost resulted in scalding-hot coffee coming out of his nose.

"Amelia, why don't you tell me how you really feel?"

"He's got a list of scandals behind him a mile long. You and I both know it. My gosh, he joked about them most of the time. You've seen him on the news."

Dan only nodded.

"That guy loved the cameras," Amelia continued. "Didn't he actually say something like *never let a good crisis go to waste* or something horribly conceited like that?" Amelia shook her head. "And everyone knew about his women. His ex-wife is probably doing cartwheels if everything she said about him after their divorce was true."

"I've got to go talk to her, too," Dan muttered, rubbing his face.

"I'm sorry, Dan. Here I am getting all riled up, and you're the one who has been up all night. Look." She stood up and took the coffee from his hand. "How about I make you a soothing tea? You can lie down on the couch and take twenty winks. It'll do you good."

Dan looked as if she had just suddenly come down with a slight case of Tourette's syndrome and spouted off a string of obscenitics to make a sailor blush.

"What?" she asked in reply to his shocked expression. "You shouldn't drive if you're tired either."

"Amelia, I think that's the best offer I've had all month. I'll take you up on that." He stood and began loosening his tie and unbuttoned his collar.

"Go on in the family room, honey, and I'll bring your tea in." She heard the word come out of her mouth too late to stop it. "I'm sorry." Her voice was breathy with embarrassment. "I used...to bring my husband tea in there. Old habits."

"No need to apologize," Dan almost whispered. "I kind of liked the sound of it."

Amelia bit her tongue to hold back the schoolgirl giggles of excitement that were running madly up her throat. Instead, she turned and put the kettle on.

Chapter Seven

Dan conked out for a solid hour on Amelia's couch. When he finally sat up, yawned, and stretched, Amelia was still at the kitchen table, calculating expenses and what she'd need to make within the next several hours at the event just to break even. There was a turkey sandwich with chips and a dill pickle across from her.

"How do you feel?" she asked.

"A world of better. I think that is the most comfortable couch I've ever slept on."

"You find yourself sleeping on them a lot, do you?"

Dan smirked and stood up, rubbing the back of his head. He had a five o'clock shadow at almost eleven in the morning. It made him look rough, manly, sexy. Amelia swallowed hard and nodded.

"I thought you might be hungry when you woke up."

It was Dan's turn to blush a little. He didn't want to admit how much like home Amelia's house felt to him. He'd never tell her how often he had thought of just stopping by after his shift was over just to see her and the kids. As it was, he rarely paid them a visit. It would be like playing house, and he didn't want that. He wanted to plant stakes. Set up housekeeping, as they would say in the old west days. But moving fast wasn't his style. It resulted in sloppy police work and an even more disastrous personal life.

"Thank you. You were right." He took a seat. While eating what he thought was the best turkey sandwich he had ever tasted, he looked at what Amelia was working on.

"How's it looking?" he asked in between a big bite of sandwich and a bite of pickle.

Amelia sighed.

"Well, it isn't the end of the world." She huffed. "In fact, if we hadn't had to pay such an obscene fee to be in our usual spot, I'd still be in the black."

"What was the fee?"

"Oh, no use worrying about it now. The city has my money, and they can use it to bury the mayor. Actually, they probably won't even use it for that. They'll use it for some stupid project like repainting the white lines in the road or naming some street after the late, great Mayor Pearl."

Dan lost himself for a moment. He reached across the table and took Amelia's hand. Squeezing it tightly, he looked into her eyes.

"It'll be okay, Amelia," he almost whispered. "And...if there is anything I can do, I hope you won't hesitate to ask me."

Amelia squeezed his hand back. Her face wrinkled into a smile she couldn't contain. Blinking her dark eyes, she opened her mouth to speak just as Adam came back up from the basement.

"Hey, Dan. I didn't know you were still here."

Slowly letting go of Amelia's hand, Dan gave Adam a wink.

"Yeah, your mom was nice enough to let me get in a quick nap on the couch. But now, I've got to get back to work." His eyes came back to Amelia and gently caressed her face. Pushing himself back from the table, he stood and buttoned his collar. Amelia stood and walked him to the door. Before he left, he turned to her, and she straightened his tie, patting it smooth and feeling his chest underneath.

"Don't eat anything from anyone you don't know."

Amelia watched him as he climbed in his car, backed out of the driveway, and drove off, tooting the horn once.

"So what did he say?" Adam asked.

"Looks like we're shut down at least for the time being. We might salvage a little of tomorrow's traffic, but it isn't looking good."

"I'm sorry, Mom."

"No worries. There isn't much we can't handle together, right?"

Adam nodded and headed upstairs to pester his sister to get out of the bathroom already.

But then Amelia's confidence slipped as she heard the wind chimes of her phone and saw that all too familiar number. "What now?" she said before pleasantly answering.

"Hi, John. What's up?"

"Have you heard about the mayor?"

"Yes." Amelia was unable to hide the sound of satisfaction in her voice.

"This is just horrible. He was such a good man." John sounded as if he were on the verge of bursting into tears.

"Yeah, okay, John. Because of the mayor's incident, they've closed down my part of the food fest event. The kids are heartbroken, and so am I. I guess the cops are scouring the area for clues."

"I just got off the phone with his wife." John completely ignored Amelia's comment. "Maggie is just beside herself."

"Yeah, I'll bet. Did you need something, John?"

Amelia was losing her patience. John had never ever cared this much about anything that had gone on in Amelia's life ever. When her father had passed away, John made sure he had a reason to leave the wake early and remained in the car on his cell phone the entire time at the cemetery. The only time she saw him actually feel any sadness was when Adam was about five, Meg was just a baby, and a cat had gotten run over in front of the house.

All the questions about animals going to heaven and won't their owner miss them and did the poor little beast suffer seemed a bit too much for the hard-hearted John, who held his son and tried to soothe his worries as best as any dad could.

"Yeah, well, I heard that you had seen an altercation between the mayor and George Pilsen's brother."

"How did you hear that?" Amelia huffed.

"Word travels fast in small circles." John sounded as if he were bragging. Amelia was sure he was. "One of the reporters who was on the scene is a friend of mine. He said he saw you there and that you saw and heard the whole thing."

"I did." Amelia chose her words carefully. "Does someone need me as a witness or something?"

"No," John snapped. "In fact, the whole thing is so ugly they'd like you to not speak to anyone about what you heard and saw. I told them I'd call and make sure you didn't."

"Really? This is coming from whom, John? Who told you this?"

"Look, we're just trying to protect the Pearl family. Maggie is all alone now and..."

"Yeah, all alone with her husband's six-figure pension and a house on a hill in addition to her summer home in the Hamptons. I'm sure she'll figure out a way to scrape by."

"Amelia, I'm not asking. I'm telling you. Do not speak to anyone about this. The detectives on the case don't need your help, and reporters don't need your version of what happened."

Amelia knew John wasn't speaking as a *real* insider. He had known of the mayor. Doing the kind of law John did, it was inevitable that some of his social circles would cross over into local politics. But he hadn't quite made it to the man's Christmas card list.

"Besides, it isn't about you. It's about the Pearl family and their loss. Show a little compassion for once."

Amelia clenched her fists. His comments made her want to hang up and dial Channel 8 News and blurt out her whole version of what took place. But then, she thought of Meg. If that hippy hot dog vendor was capable of killing the mayor just minutes after making lewd comments to her fifteen-year-old daughter, there was no telling what he might do if he tied the two together.

"Promise you won't talk to anyone. Amelia? Can I trust you?"

"I was never the one whose trust was called into question," she stated, enjoying one small zing regarding his infidelity. She took a deep breath, letting it out as she tossed her head back.

"Good enough. Jennifer and I are going to the funeral. It's the day after tomorrow. I'll send a bouquet on behalf of you and the kids."

"Send it from the kids. I didn't vote for the man." Amelia looked at her watch. "I've got to go, John. Is there anything else?"

John quickly wrapped up his end of the conversation. As usual, he didn't ask about The Pink Cupcake, the food fest, or anything that had to do with her life but made sure she remembered to have the kids ready on time for his next visit.

Her mind began to click as she wondered why John would make such a phone call. It was odd even for him.

Grabbing her laptop, she began reviewing the local news. The death of Mayor Pearl was all over the place. There were pictures of him smiling and laughing, shaking hands with voters, and being a man of the people.

Anyone who wasn't from the town of Gary would think he looked like the most honest fellow you could buy a used car from and after the transaction have a beer with.

But there was nothing about the altercation with the hot dog vendor. The article mentioned the mayor going to Gary Food Fest. It stated he enjoyed samples of the local cuisine. It sounded as if he'd had a great time up until the very end.

"That's weird," Amelia mumbled. "All those reporters around. Not a snapshot. Not a blurb. Nothing about the argument."

Then a strange line caught Amelia's attention.

The mayor's ex-wife could not be reached for comment.

"Sure. She probably doesn't want to incriminate herself. I can only imagine the stories that old Babs Montgomery-Pearl would weave about her late ex-husband." Amelia closed up the computer and stared into space for a few minutes.

Barbara "Babs" Montgomery-Pearl had been married to Mayor Pearl for as long as Amelia could remember. As with so many divorce stories, the mayor had gotten tired of the woman who'd supported him at the very beginning of his career when he had nothing. So when it was obvious he had acquired *everything*, he dumped Babs for, surprisingly, an only slightly younger model. That was Maggie.

It was also well known that part of the divorce agreement required Babs to keep her mouth shut about all things.

"I wonder what her allowance was for that," Amelia mused again. "I wonder if it applies if the guy is dead."

Maybe it did since the woman couldn't be reached for comment. Unless she had her own version of John calling to tell her not to talk. To think of the poor grieving family and let bygones be bygones.

Amelia shook her head and stood from the table. She was going stir crazy. It was the frustration at not being able to bake and sell her cupcakes—the worry over having dumped so much money into an event she couldn't even participate in had taken its toll on her.

"I've got to do something to keep busy," she grumbled.

She called both kids and told them she was going to go to the truck and clean things up and see if there was any news about when they'd be back in business.

Meg requested to be dropped off at Katherine's house. Adam said he would enjoy the solitude of his basement lair and fix himself a sandwich if he got hungry later.

Within an hour, Amelia was at The Pink Cupcake. She knew it was just a truck, but its hot-pink color made it stand out so that Amelia thought it looked like a pretty thing that had gotten stood up for prom.

"You had the same idea as me?" She heard a familiar male voice to her right.

"Hi, Gavin. Yeah." Amelia sighed. "This is a real blow." Her hand went to the nape of her neck, and she smoothed her hair.

"Right? The guy didn't even eat any of our food. I just don't understand this."

Amelia nodded.

"I don't even know what I'm doing here. They said they'd call if we were going to be able to open up again. I guess I just thought if I showed up, maybe..."

"Maybe they'd let us open up?" Amelia finished Gavin's sentence. "Yeah. I just don't like leaving my truck here. I don't trust anyone around her."

"Her?" Gavin said teasingly.

"Yeah, her. My daughter picked the color, the name. The Pink Cupcake is definitely a 'her.'"

Gavin laughed and looked out at the police who were standing and talking at the perimeter of the yellow DO NOT CROSS tape, then down at his shoes.

"Hey, it's almost lunchtime. Would you like to grab something to eat while we're killing time?"

Amelia, who realized she hadn't eaten anything all morning, suddenly felt a pang in her stomach. Lila's advice quickly flew through her mind. Before she could stop herself, she nodded.

"Sure."

Chapter Eight

La Café was a small Mexican restaurant just around the corner from Food Truck Alley. The place had three Formica tables and did a ton of carryout. Amelia and Gavin took a seat by the window.

Before Amelia even realized what was happening, she was laughing and smiling, telling stories about her kids and Lila.

"My question is," Gavin said, "why cupcakes?"

"Well"–Amelia frowned while chewing a mouthful of chicken burrito–"why did you pick Philly Cheese Steaks?"

"Because I am actually from Philadelphia." Gavin smirked.

"My kids always liked it when I baked for them. They said that my cupcakes were way better than any of the ones the other kids' moms brought for their birthdays or class parties."

"Is that all?"

Amelia wiped her mouth with the paper napkin.

"I'm good at it. It's just one of those weird gifts. I feel comfortable in the kitchen. I know women aren't supposed to say that anymore, but its true. When I'm baking something, I'm in charge. I'm the boss. I'd never been the boss before."

Gavin smiled. He had a very handsome face, and Amelia could tell that he took care to stay in shape. But she wasn't sure if there was a connection there. Not yet. She looked at his bright-blue eyes, which reminded her of Paul Newman's, but quickly looked away.

"Why are you blushing?" he asked eagerly.

"I don't like to talk about myself. I'd rather talk about my kids. Or Lila. She's a stitch."

Gavin slowly nodded as his eyes seemed to feel their way over Amelia's facial features and down her neck.

Feeling a little awkward, Amelia proceeded to tell Gavin about how she and

Lila came together and babbled on that Lila was responsible for her hugely successful PB&J cupcakes.

By the time lunch was over, Amelia felt exhausted. She knew she had talked too much, but she was nervous. Gavin probably thought she was some kind of lunatic.

"I really had a nice time with you, Amelia," he said as they walked back to Food Truck Alley.

"Me, too," Amelia chirped. "But I wish you would have let me pay for my own lunch. I'm not destitute yet."

"Call me old fashioned. I invited you. It was my pleasure."

As they rounded the corner, Amelia saw a familiar face by The Pink Cupcake.

"That's Officer Miller over there." She pointed. "I provided the cupcakes at her bridal shower. She must be back from her honeymoon. So I guess she isn't Officer Miller anymore."

"Hey, let me know if she has any news about when we can get cooking again," Gavin said. "And let me know when you are free for dinner. I'd love to take you to this great Italian place over on the south side."

Amelia smiled, only half hearing what Gavin had said, and turned to him with her hand extended.

"I'll do that." She felt his warm hand almost completely engulfing hers. "Thanks again for lunch. I had a really nice time."

Leaving him to find his way back to the Philly Cheese Steak mobile, Amelia quickly hustled up to Officer Miller.

"Darcy!" she called, waving. The officer smiled broadly and waved back.

"I was just looking for you." Darcy straightened her belt, which held her weapon, cuffs, mace, and who knew what other law enforcing trinkets in hidden pouches.

"Oh yeah? What for?" Amelia prayed that it was to tell her they'd be reopening the trucks within the next fifteen minutes.

"Can you tell me about what happened yesterday with the fellow who yelled at the mayor?"

Amelia's thoughts went to her ex-husband's bizarre request.

"Well, I already gave a statement to Detective Walishovsky. Both Lila and I told him everything yesterday."

"Yeah, he told me that. But now it looks like all his notes that he typed up for the file are missing. His handwritten ones were torn out of his pad."

"Could they be misplaced or..." Her words sounded like a pitiful excuse a child might give a teacher when they didn't do their homework.

"We're talking about Detective Walishovsky."

Nodding, Amelia put her hand up as if to say, "Yeah. Stupid to ask." If it was to help Dan, Amelia had no problem repeating everything she had said yesterday. Darcy wrote down the notes quickly and then stuffed them deep inside her jacket pocket.

"Darcy, do you have any idea when we might be able to get back to work?"

Amelia sighed. It was like a broken record in her head. *When are we getting back to work...when are we getting back to work...*

"They haven't said anything yet. They've put up a grid." Darcy pointed to the small stakes tied together with string making tiny squares along the grass. "Once they make it through each square, I suppose then they'll open things back up. They are about halfway through."

"Do me a favor," Amelia whispered. "Crack the whip. I need to get back to work."

Darcy smiled and gave Amelia a wink. "I'll do my best. In the meantime, there might be another catering job for you in the near future if you're interested."

"You've got my number." Amelia nodded.

She watched as Darcy walked back toward the officers standing at the yellow caution tape. Darcy issued a few orders, to which the men turned and told the guys on the ground to pick up the pace.

Gavin leaned out the back of his truck and gave her a questioning glance. Amelia shook her head and shrugged. No news.

Sure, she could have stayed with The Pink Cupcake, but it was locked up tight, and with so many uniforms around, it was probably as safe as it would have been in the driveway. Instead, she decided to go for a drive and clear her head.

Dan must have gone ballistic after realizing his paperwork was missing. Who would do that and why? Why didn't anyone want to know about this guy? Why wasn't the press reporting about him and asking for anyone and everyone with information about him to come forward? What kind of people were these?

What was really frightening was that John was also involved. Did he know that the police report had been messed with?

"He couldn't have. Darcy seemed to insinuate that was private information," Amelia said to the steering wheel of her sedan. "What kind of people are these exactly? Someone knows this guy, I'll bet."

The funeral.

"That's it. I'll go to the wake and the funeral. If they don't let me in, I'll just watch the place. I can do that. I've done stakeouts before. But if John is involved with these people and they are messing with Dan's work..." She didn't know what else to say. Did she think she could take on city hall?

Turning her car around, she headed back home. Calling Meg on her cell and Adam at home, she made sure they were okay, stopped at Pizza Hut, and brought home an early dinner.

Then, getting back on the computer, she found out all the details of the wake that was taking place tomorrow. Luckily, she had a black dress that still fit. Amelia opted for a pair of flat black shoes. For some reason, she thought there might be a chance she'd have to run off on foot. Heels would not be a good idea. Her binoculars would fit perfectly in her clutch purse.

"Girl, you infiltrated an Gamblers Anonymous meeting without being noticed. You've got this," she said to cheer herself on, nodding and smiling as if she were doing nothing more than crashing a party.

But these are politicians, not a bunch of recovering gamblers.

Pushing the words aside, Amelia pretended not to have heard her thoughts.

Chapter Nine

Hughes Funeral Chapel was in the prestigious Bridgeport suburb that was as far away from downtown Gary as you could get but still be in the district for voting purposes. Bridgeport was also the home of the late Mayor Pearl and his second wife, Maggie. Those streets were the first to be plowed after a snowfall, the first for the sweepers to sweep every Wednesday, all the residents always received their mail, and with so many retired police living there, too, the most severe crime reported all last year was vandalism. Some kids spray-painted NO REGRET on the overpass at I-394 and Sauk Trail.

Not all the homes were as prestigious looking as the mayor's. He did live on a hill, and his neighbors had huge houses and large pieces of land. But the majority of the homes were simple middle-class-looking ranch-style homes. The yards were clean. The cars in the driveway were huge Chevy trucks or Cadillac SUVs.

Shaking her head as she drove, Amelia thought it all had a film over it. Something dirty.

"You're just saying that because you hate the mayor and all politicians," she said scoldingly to herself. "These are normal people. Just doing their jobs." But she couldn't shake the feeling that not only were things different in Bridgeport, but she was being watched.

Casually, she scanned the fronts of the homes. Sure enough, many of them had surveillance cameras.

"Surveillance cameras for these simple homes?" she muttered. Shaking her head, she slipped on her sunglasses, tried not to stare, and followed the directions to Hughes Funeral Chapel.

Before she could even get on the same block, she was stopped at a roadblock.

Rolling down her window, she leaned out to get the attention of the officer who was directing traffic.

"Hi." She tried to sound natural. "I'm trying to get to the Hughes Funeral Home."

"Sorry, ma'am. The road is blocked to all thru traffic. Do you have a pass?"

"A pass?"

The officer's face looked tired, as if he had already repeated what he had said a thousand times and it wasn't even nine in the morning yet.

"Only police, press, and immediate family and friends are allowed past the barricades." He looked over her car. It was obvious she was the least interesting thing around.

"Oh, um, well, I was supposed to meet Detective Walishovsky here?" She swallowed hard. What was she doing? Under the pressure, his was the first name to pop into her head. Detective Dan "Strictly by the books" Walishovsky was going to have kittens if he found out about this.

The police officer let out a sigh.

"Okay, go around this block and park your car there. You'll have to walk through." He shook his head with frustration.

Amelia did as she was told. After parking her car and quickly hurrying back to the barricade, she saw the officer standing alone at the orange-and-white roadblock. This blew her chance of surveillance from a distance. She couldn't very well stand across the street staring through binoculars at who was coming and going.

Almost on tiptoe, she hurried past the blockade and made her way to the funeral home. The next obstacle would be getting into the place itself. Slowing down her pace, she pretended to be looking at her phone and having a quiet conversation as she watched the cars that were allowed to pull past the roadblocks from the opposite direction of the street.

Almost every one was a limousine. There were large men stationed at the door and casually strolling through the parking lot. They didn't look like regular policemen in civilian clothes. These guys were melon thumpers. Kneecap breakers. They were the same kind of guys that had surrounded the mayor at the food fest. Amelia wondered why Maggie would approve these guys to patrol the guests of her late husband's funeral when they didn't do much good protecting him in the first place.

Watching and waiting, still unnoticed, Amelia saw her chance. A limousine pulled up and unloaded over twelve people. It was like a clown car, and they just kept coming and coming.

Quickly putting away her phone, she pulled a handkerchief from her sleeve, held it under her sunglasses, and simply walked in with the group.

Her heart was pounding madly in her chest. She was sure that within seconds a big, meaty hand attached to one of those bouncers was going to clamp down on her shoulder. She'd be tossed out not before half a dozen reporters snapped her picture. The headlines would be frame worthy.

"Owner of Pink Cupcake Food Truck Thrown from Mayor's Funeral"

But, while she held her breath and walked farther from the door she'd just passed through, she realized no one saw her. No one was paying any attention to her.

She wanted to smile. This was the most exciting thing she had ever done. Drifting through the crowd, she took note of all the designer handbags, thousand-dollar dresses, tailored suits, and gorgeous jewelry the mourners were wearing. She saw several television anchormen. There were half a dozen aldermen and their wives that Amelia had seen in the newspaper but didn't know their names. Flowers were arranged, taking up half the room, from the teamsters union, County Hospital, Fire Station #9, the Fraternal Order of Police, and the list went on. Before Amelia knew what was happening, she was in the receiving line to offer her condolences to Widow Pearl.

Her mouth went dry. Surely this woman would take one look at Amelia and scream or point at her. "Imposter!" she'd yell or "Funeral crasher!" or something equally humiliating.

Before she could turn tail and run, Maggie Pearl was looking at her with red-rimmed eyes and waiting.

Without thinking, Amelia walked up to Maggie Pearl, extended her hand, and felt tears well in her own eyes. The woman looked tired. She didn't look at all like Amelia thought a wealthy, kept woman would look. There was barely any makeup on her face. Whether she had cried it all off or hadn't bothered to put any on, Amelia couldn't tell. She had a round face that was plump and pleasant. Her eyes were hazel in a sea of red puffiness. A kind smile spread across her face.

"I'm so sorry for your loss, Maggie," Amelia managed to choke out.

"Thank you so much." Maggie replied quietly, taking both Amelia's hands in hers. "Who would do this to him? You know, he loved this city. He did the best he knew how."

Did she know? Amelia felt her mouth dry up, so she nodded, squeezing Maggie's hand before letting go and walking toward the closed casket to pay her respects to the deceased.

This was a horrible idea. What was she thinking? Suddenly, there was a very human face on this situation, and Amelia wasn't prepared. Tears filled her eyes, but she bit the inside of her cheek, making them retreat back into her tear ducts.

Did she know? Did Maggie Pearl know I hated the mayor? Did she know I thought all politicians were crooks and Mayor Richard M. Pearl in particular? How could she?

She knelt down in front of the casket as she had done at her own parents' funerals. She folded her hands and said a quick prayer, not for the mayor, but for Maggie.

As she crossed herself and began to stand, she had completely forgotten about the fear of being thrown out until she felt a hand slip under her arm, squeezing tightly, almost yanking her to her feet.

"What are you doing here?" the voice hissed in her ear. She knew that voice.

Chapter Ten

"John?" She turned to see her ex-husband towering over her.

"How did you get in here?"

"I walked, thank you," Amelia snapped, yanking her arm from his clutch. "I can come and offer my condolences as a taxpayer. No one said I couldn't."

John looked around as if afraid of being seen. He ran his hand over his mouth and smacked his lips.

"All right. You've paid your respects. Now, go home." His voice was low and almost a whisper but had the intensity of a cracking whip.

Not wanting to attract any attention to herself, Amelia straightened her skirt, tucked her clutch under her arm, and began to walk toward the exit at the back of the room. More and more people were coming in. Before long, there would be such a big crowd John wouldn't know if she had actually left or not.

Stepping into the hallway, Amelia saw her lifeboat in this sea of social climbers. Ladies' Powder Room.

Once inside, she let out a deep breath. There were several women inside, chitchatting amongst themselves, giving Amelia a pleasant nod as she walked in. They didn't know who she was, and they didn't seem to care.

The room had the feel of a giant powder puff. The chaise lounge and loveseats seemed to be extra poufy, and the lighting made all the women look as if they were in old black-and-white films and the camera lenses had a thin layer of Vaseline smeared on them. And on every flat surface was a tissue box ready to be plucked like a weird flower.

There was another more brightly lit area where the bathroom stalls were located. Just as Amelia had the idea to go plant herself in one of the private stalls to let a little time pass, another familiar face appeared. Jennifer.

Rolling her eyes and turning her back quickly, Amelia now saw what was really driving John to get her out of the building. He'd brought Jennifer with him.

Amelia watched her as she washed her hands in the sink. She was wearing leopard-print shoes with her black dress.

"Good grief." Amelia muttered, turning away. Shoes like that were meant for dinner and dancing. Not a funeral. It was petty, of course, but hadn't the girl's mother taught her anything?

Apparently not if she stole your husband. Amelia shrugged. Standing next to a small mirror, Amelia looked at her own reflection and smoothed her hair down. Looking behind her, she kept an eye on Jennifer, who was carefully fixing her makeup.

Finally, satisfied with any touch-ups, Jennifer turned and walked out of the room. Several of the older women watched her go by, and Amelia listened to what they had to say after she passed.

It was strange, but Amelia was relieved they didn't make any comments about her.

To them, she was just a younger woman at a funeral. She wasn't a home-wrecker or adulteress. Heck, with all the politicians crammed inside this structure, Amelia was sure she was in the minority of people who had never cheated on a spouse.

Rubbing her forehead, confident she was now in a room full of strangers, she sat in a corner chair by a window that looked out to the alley behind the building. The parking lot stretched back there and was filled with cars, all tagged with the special orange sticker reading FUNERAL on it.

"I can't say I'm surprised about this."

The words came from a full-figured dame to Amelia's right. Her eye makeup was as dramatic as Cleopatra's, and she waved her manicured hands around as she spoke. She was sitting with a rail-thin elderly woman who, although she was pale and wrinkled, looked very classy in a conservative navy-blue suit with a little American flag on the lapel.

"You did predict it," the elderly woman said. "I remember."

"You can't be up to your knees in mud and not expect to get your hands dirty," Cleopatra added. "He had that Bringham

Corner thing. He had, what was it called, Overshore..."

"Oftenshore, yes. Yes," the older woman offered, her eyes widening.

"And we can't forget Linda." Cleopatra shook her head.

"We couldn't if we tried."

Linda Watkins-Pearl, or Linda Watkins, as she was now the ex-wife of the late mayor, came from a political family.

"They propped him up. I know it isn't right to speak badly about the dead, but without her, everyone would be saying, 'Richard M. Who?,'" the elderly woman added.

Amelia leaned a little to the right to hear the conversation.

"Is she coming today?" the older lady continued.

"I'd be shocked if she didn't. Linda's never been one to shy away from cameras and controversy. I'm sure she's got an opinion about what happened, and I wouldn't put it past her to name names."

"I wouldn't put it past her to have her hands in some of that mud, too."

Amelia froze.

"Come on." Cleopatra stood, holding her hand out to her friend. "We better get back out there before they wonder what we're up to."

"You're right. I'll say this is the driest funeral I've ever been to." The older woman stuffed a handkerchief in her clutch. "The only one crying is Maggie."

"That poor thing is too dumb to realize this is a blessing in disguise."

Amelia held her breath as the women stood, and then let out a long, noisy breath when they finally exited the powder room.

"The ex-wife," she mumbled to herself. "That's a suspect and a half."

Standing up, she straightened her dress, checked her face in the mirror, then looked at her watch. Enough time had gone by that John would believe she'd left. She slowly pulled the door open and searched for any familiar faces. She saw none.

She merged with the crowd and began to weave her way through the people. It gave her the feeling that she was a tiny germ looking to infiltrate a much bigger organism. She circled around and listened to bits and pieces of conversation, shocked at what she was hearing.

"Did you see the game last night..."

"I was able to book tee time for three o'clock today. It's a little late, but..."

"We are going to the dinner at Lulu and Stiles's place..."

"How is your daughter liking college..."

People were talking about everything and anything but the dead man in the casket. What kind of bizarro world was this? Amelia held her composure and made her way to the small kitchen, where she slipped in unnoticed, poured herself a small paper cup of coffee, then stepped back out into the hallway to sip it. She took out her cell phone and held it to her ear, pretending to be in a serious conversation.

It was then that she saw the trio of large men coming in her direction.

Bouncers! her mind screamed. *This is going to be a hundred shades of humiliation.*

She stared at them as they approached. Each man looked as if they could have played professional football. One man was black and wore a goatee and a gold pinky ring. The one in the middle was completely bald but had thick eyebrows and deep-set eyes, making him look like a very dangerous Kewpie doll. The third one had sandy-brown hair cut close at the sides and a little longer on top. His eyes were narrow. He was speaking to the other two men, but you couldn't see his teeth when his lips moved.

Standing rail straight, Amelia was sure her heart was beating loud enough for them to hear. If not, they would surely see the sweat that had broken out over her forehead.

Would they grab her? Should she set her coffee down? Would she be paraded through the front lobby in front of everyone, or would they discreetly shove her out into the alley to avoid a scene?

"Ma'am." The black guard nodded as he walked past and into the kitchen with the rest of them.

She looked behind her at the wall, down on the floor, then up again, putting her phone back to her ear.

They just wanted some coffee. She peeked into the small kitchen, which was now filled to capacity with just those three men. A few of the people who had been sitting at the small table excused themselves, obviously feeling claustrophobic, and gave the bouncers the room to themselves.

It wasn't long before the conversation turned toward the late mayor.

"The only bad thing about this is finding a new job," the bald guard whined.

"You think?" the black guard replied. "We get a year's compensation, and that's plenty of time to find a new job. I'm taking a yearlong vacation."

"It'll take a year," Baldy chirped, obviously the pessimist in the group. "Our resumes are tainted because of this guy. It may not be all that easy to find another gig."

"Are you kidding?" The black guard was not convinced. "All these types got secrets to hide. You know, I once rode security for the mother of the governor of Illinois. The man's eighty-eight-year-old mother, and she was paying off reporters to make sure they didn't ask her son about some public school project that he was stealing money from. His own mother." He chuckled as he told the story. "These kinds of people always want protection. Even if they don't, they want to *look* like they need it. Makes 'em feel important."

"I never had a problem with Maggie. But I'll tell you what." The bald guard lowered his voice. "I'm glad someone finally put an end to this SOB. And don't tell me you guys aren't thinking the same."

"How can you say that?" Amelia heard the last guard with the blond hair finally speak. He sounded agitated. "The man hasn't been dead a week. Show a little respect."

"Chuck?" The black guard was almost laughing. "Is that you talking, or have aliens replaced your body with a pod?"

"I'm completely serious. They don't know who did this to him, and you guys should be a little more concerned about that. In fact, if you were doing what you were paid to do, maybe this *wouldn't* have happened."

"Look." The bald bodyguard sounded mad. "I'm not going to pretend Richard M. Pearl was some kind of saint just because karma finally caught up with him. And you, Chuck, should remember how he treated all of us, especially yourself. Because I can't say he didn't get what he had coming to him."

"He didn't treat me any differently than…"

"Who are you talking to?" Baldy snapped. "He enjoyed taking you down a notch."

"Yeah," the black guard concurred. "Whatever it was about you, he seemed to take an extra interest in. Did you ever figure it out?"

"I'm not going to talk about that. It's all over and done with. Life is too short."

"Sorry, Chuck," Baldy added. "I'm glad the man is dead. Time to move on. Find some young, single model type with her own reality show to protect. At least the view will be better."

"I think you're wrong. And you better hope nobody asks me what you really thought of the guy when they dig deep in the investigation," Chuck snapped.

"Are you threatening me?" The bald guard was raising his voice.

"No. I'm just being honest."

"Wait a minute. Come on, you two." The black guard seemed to be the only level-headed one at the moment. Amelia held her breath and listened. "They are digging into the people who served him food at the food fest. None of us are suspects. So no need for us to turn on each other."

This was all interesting talk, and Amelia wanted to stay and listen as long as she could, but then she saw the man at the end of the hall staring at her.

Chapter Eleven

"Amelia?" Dan looked puzzled, yet something twinkled in his eyes as if he was telling himself he shouldn't be surprised to see her at the mayor's standing-room-only funeral.

All the voices in the kitchen stopped. Without turning to look behind her, Amelia walked confidently out of the corner she had been standing in the whole time and up to Dan. She was glad it was him and not her ex-husband. But she could feel the three sets of eyes watching her and whispering, wondering if she had heard everything they had said.

"Hello, Detective." She smoothed the back of her neck. "Had I known you were coming to this, I wouldn't have gone through the trouble of sneaking in."

"How long have you been here?" He looked at her outfit then back at her face.

"Long enough to know no one but Maggie Pearl seems upset the mayor was murdered," she whispered. "How about you?"

"I'm beginning to come to the same conclusion." Dan squinted at the bodyguards, who were looking at them from the kitchen. Amelia, still not daring to turn around, slipped her hand around Dan's elbow.

"Maybe we should go somewhere else to talk." She looked at Dan, jerking her head slightly toward the three-man audience watching them. Dan understood, and as Amelia pretended to dab her eyes with the tissue in her hand, he led her down the hallway and into the main lobby.

Finding a quiet corner, they stood together in view of everyone yet still not being noticed.

"I heard your files on the mayor's death were missing," Amelia mentioned to Dan as they walked out of the wake. "That's pretty out of the ordinary to happen at a police station, isn't it?"

"It never happens," he grumbled. "Can I ask how you got into this circus?"

"I just acted as if I belonged." She smiled up at him.

Amelia quickly told Dan what the women in the restroom had said and also mentioned the bodyguards and their list of complaints and comments. When she mentioned the state of Maggie Pearl, Dan slumped against the back of the seat.

"You met Maggie Pearl?"

"Well, I wouldn't say *met her*, but I shook her hand and told her I was sorry. I don't get the impression she had anything to do with it. That is my official opinion as a baker."

Dan ran his hand through his hair.

"I couldn't get within ten feet of Maggie Pearl." He smirked. "What is it about you, Amelia, that makes everyone you meet feel they can trust you?"

Amelia took a deep breath and held it, trying to find a sarcastic remark or playful reply, but all she could come up with was a simple shrug.

"So let me tell you what I heard..."

Amelia was almost gushing with excitement, when everything was cut short as a wild number of photographers collided with security at the main entrance.

"What the..." Even Dan was shocked, and nothing usually rattled his cage.

Bursting through the door wearing a black full-length fur coat and red high heels was Linda Watkins, the ex-wife of the late Mayor Pearl.

"I have every right to be here!" she shouted, wobbling a little on her heels.

"Is she...?" Amelia put her hand to her throat.

"Drunk? I think that's a safe bet," Dan replied.

Crossing one foot awkwardly in front of the other, Linda proceeded to make her way across the lobby before she was stopped not five feet in front of Amelia and Dan by Mr. Gimbroni, the funeral director.

"Mrs. Watkins. What are you doing here? We discussed our arrangement yesterday, and you agreed...."

"I didn't agree to anything," she hissed. "That man in there got what he deserved.

And I always said if I outlived him, I'd show up at his funeral in a red dress and dance..."

"Mrs. Watkins, you're making a scene." Mr. Gimbroni was trying to calm the woman down, but it was not working.

"Making a scene? Ha! You haven't seen anything yet!" she hollered. "I loved him! I practically handed city hall over to him on a platter! And what was the thanks I got? Divorce papers on my birthday!"

"Ouch." Amelia shook her head. It was inappropriate and maybe even cruel, but Amelia couldn't say she didn't know exactly how Mrs. Watkins was feeling. In fact, hearing those words reminded her that her own ex-husband was still somewhere in the building. As she looked around, she nearly jumped as her eyes locked with John's.

She could tell he was furious she was still there. But as Mrs. Watkins continued to air her dirty laundry about the mayor's affairs, his lies to her, and those his new wife was bound to discover, she narrowed her eyes and shook her head. How pathetically similar their two men were.

It must have been an obvious comparison, because John looked away first.

"I'm not leaving until I get my time alone with him!" she shouted at poor Mr. Gimbroni, who just wanted to proceed with the wake. Taking Mrs. Watkins's hands in his, he lowered his voice and said what were obviously some soothing things, to which she nodded then dabbed her eyes with a handkerchief as she allowed him to lead her to a small room that was down a short hallway and off his office.

He emerged alone, apologizing to the crowd, to which everyone nodded and shook their heads at the poor guy, who had not expected such an outburst at the most notorious funeral at his establishment in years. It was sort of stupid of him to think there wouldn't be a whole drama meltdown at this event, Amelia thought.

People went back to their socializing, shaking hands, and making their way toward the room where Maggie was blissfully unaware of the scene that had just taken place—at least until some "do-gooder" decided to tell her about it.

"That was interesting," Dan mumbled.

"Wait here." Amelia let go of his arm and casually walked toward the small hallway. Stopping at the water dispenser along the wall, she filled a little cup, smoothed the front of her dress, and walked into the little room off Mr. Gimbroni's office and shut the door behind her.

Amelia was sure Dan was waiting to hear some furniture being thrown along with a string of obscenities from the woman, but it was worse. It was deathly quiet.

Swallowing hard, Amelia approached Linda Watkins, who had taken a seat by a small window and was staring out at the view of the alley.

She turned and looked at Amelia, swaying just a little as the alcohol in her system started to wear off due to the rush of adrenaline she'd experienced.

"Hi." Amelia cleared her throat but spoke as if she were speaking to one of her kids when they were sick. "I thought you might like a drink of water. It's overwhelming out there." She extended her hand holding the little white cup.

Linda Watkins looked at Amelia's hand then up at her face.

Amelia watched as the woman swayed slightly in her seat until she finally took the cup and took a sip.

"Thank you." Linda nodded.

Amelia smiled and turned to walk away.

"Who are you?"

Before she could leave the room, Amelia turned and faced the late mayor's ex-wife.

"My name is Amelia. I didn't know the mayor. I'm just here to pay my respects with a friend."

"You didn't know him? That explains how you can smile." Linda took her leather clutch purse off her shoulder, opened it, and pulled out a pack of cigarettes. "I gave that man my best years. And what did he do?"

Amelia shook her head, walked over to the window, unlocked it, and slid it up so the smoke would go outside.

"He took them, like he took the land deals my father arranged for him, like he took the precinct realignments, like he took the family contract jobs, all of it, and put them in his pockets. Stuffed them, like a little kid with a dollar at a penny candy store." She took a deep drag and let the smoke blast from her nostrils. "Are you in politics? I don't think I've ever seen you before." Linda squinted at her.

"No. Not at all. I'm just a registered voter."

Linda let out a loud quack of a laugh.

"Good for you. They can't be trusted. Not a single one of them." She pointed a French-manicured nail toward the door. "Between you and me"—she leaned closer to Amelia, who could smell the liquor on her breath—"I knew this was going to happen."

"You did?" Amelia leaned against the windowsill and watched as Linda pulled a small flask from her clutch purse. There seemed to be a bottomless supply of little helpers in there. Unscrewing the top, she offered a nip to Amelia, who shook her head no.

With a shrug, Linda took a quick swig and stared out the window.

"I knew it was all going to catch up with him. My father..." she began but started to cry. "My father was a great man. He helped Richard get started because my father, see, had a lot of connections." She placed her index finger on the side of her nose. "Connections?"

Amelia nodded. She was sure she had seen that signal in a movie about the mafia once but couldn't be sure. Either way, she was pretty confident she knew what Linda meant.

"When he divorced me, he didn't just break my heart. He broke my father's heart, too. He treated him like his own son. Gave him every opportunity."

"Sometimes men don't see what they have until it's too late." Amelia couldn't think of anything else to say. She knew it wasn't comforting or even all that helpful. But she said it.

"No. But I'll guarantee he saw me before he died. He saw me and my father and everyone else he took from. But especially me because I put a..."

"Is someone smoking in here?"

Mr. Gimbroni burst into the room, surprised to see Amelia talking with the late mayor's ex-wife.

"Ma'am, I'm going to have to ask you to leave."

Amelia nodded as Linda gave her a wave while taking another deep drag off her cigarette.

As she stepped out of the room, she could hear Mr. Gimbroni trying to get Linda to put out her smoke.

"Good luck." Amelia hummed to herself. She spotted Dan still standing in the corner she had left him in. His left eyebrow shot up into his forehead, making her feel a flutter in her stomach.

"I don't believe you." He shook his head.

"Believe it or not, Detective, that woman was in need of a shoulder to lean on."

"And did she?"

"Oh, you aren't going to believe what I've got to tell you."

"Yeah, well, that makes two of us, but not here. What do you say we head over to the coffee shop down the street?"

Amelia nodded, and Dan gave her a wink that made her smile. It was inappropriate to smile so widely at a funeral, but she couldn't help it. On her way out, she was sure she saw John and Jennifer speaking with some gray-haired man in a pinstriped suit and his wife. Both people were old enough to be Jennifer's grandparents.

"Isn't that your ex-husband?" Dan asked in that serious, matter-of-fact way he asked questions.

"Yes" was enough of an answer. She was sure she'd get a tongue-lashing the next time John called about how rude it was to crash funerals and what would have happened had Jennifer seen her. It wasn't the funeral John was worried about. It was *John*, as usual. But Amelia knew where she was. She knew exactly what she was doing. Perhaps that was why she was so surprised when the fresh air outside made her think about Maggie Pearl and Linda Watkins. Both of them were hurting due to the very different acts of the same man. And that man was dead as a result of his actions against...someone.

The pair snuck around the building and out of earshot of any mourners, security, and press. There, Amelia told Dan that an intoxicated Linda Watkins had practically confessed to doing something to her ex-husband that contributed to his death.

"At least, that is what I get out of it. What do you think?" Amelia looked at Dan like a student feeling they had asked their professor the dumbest question ever asked in the history of questions.

"I think we might want to wait a while until Mrs. Watkins has paid her respects. Follow me."

Across the street from Hughes Funeral Home was a pawnshop. The neon light indicated they bought gold and paid cash. Inside, the place smelled of cigarette smoke. The glass counters displayed the easily moved merchandise like cameras, sunglasses, jewelry, and watches. Stereo equipment, fur and leather coats, and several rifles were behind the counters and behind a sliding metal gate for extra security.

The proprietor looked at the pair as they loitered by the door, watching the bustle across the street.

"That's her car." Dan pointed to a sleek navy-blue Lincoln with a man waiting behind the wheel with a newspaper spread out in front of him.

"Are you sure?" Amelia asked. "They all look alike to me."

"I'm sure." Dan took out a tiny set of binoculars. "Yup. I've busted her driver before."

Amelia's jaw fell open.

"Drugs. He threw Watkins's name at me, and before I could book him, he had some slick, fast-talking lawyer at the station basically making a deal of probation or community service. Something." Dan clicked his tongue.

"I don't know if I'd want a guy who did drugs driving me around," Amelia mused as she looked toward the car.

"They have some kind of special arrangement, I'm sure."

"Hey! You two gonna buy anything?" the pawnshop owner cawed from behind the farthest glass counter at the other end of the shore. He had protruding eyes and wore a gold chain around his neck that had to be a quarter of an inch thick. It was a terrible accessory to his teal-colored button-down cabana shirt.

Dan pulled out his badge and flashed it quickly, making the man roll his eyes and flop his arms at his sides.

"Hey, everything in here has tags and receipts. Nothing stolen. I run an honest business here."

"That's good to know," Dan snapped back. "We might be here for a while." He looked down at Amelia. "Take a look around. Maybe you'll see something you'll like."

Amelia had never been in a pawnshop and wasn't sure what the proper procedure was. But curiosity got the best of her, and she walked up to the glass display case in the middle of the room that held some beautifully gaudy vintage jewelry. What had prompted the owners to get rid of these things, she wondered. Were they desperate, or were they indifferent?

This whole storefront was a collection of mysteries. People had their reasons for getting rid of things but wanted no questions asked. Mr. Gold Chain had to stay in business, so no questions ever were asked.

All the intrigue had Amelia wishing someone would come in and make a transaction just so she could see how it was done.

"Looks like we're moving," Dan called to Amelia.

"That didn't take long."

"No. And we have to be careful. It looks like she's getting an escort out."

Amelia rushed to the door to see the sandy-headed bouncer she had seen in the small kitchenette leading Linda Watkins roughly to her car.

"They look like they know each other," Amelia murmured. Just their body language made it clear that Linda was not being thrown out of the wake by a complete stranger.

As she hobbled to her car, the driver quickly folded up the paper and set it aside to jump up and open the door. Dan quickly dashed out of the pawnshop and approached the ex-wife of the late mayor.

Amelia hung back, watching from the sidewalk. She could hear Linda Watkins loudly chastising the Pearl family, the alderman in attendance, the city workers who were there, and the civilians. It was obvious she was still a little drunk.

Dan showed his badge as he approached her. It impressed Amelia that Linda made no effort to run away or call Dan any names. In fact, she seemed happy to talk to him. Too happy, as she squeezed his arm, touched his chest as she spoke, looked him up and down, and smiled madly.

"I can't blame her," Amelia complained. Dan was a good-looking man. It probably came in handy when working with lonely widows and vengeful divorcees. Yikes, was that what she was...a vengeful divorcee?

Before Amelia could analyze her own behavior, she saw Dan shake hands with Linda, who pulled him closer to give him a hug and pat him on the back before he turned and headed back to the pawn shop.

Amelia ducked back from the door and waited for him to step inside.

"What did she say? Did she tell you what she told me?"

"Yes." Dan turned and looked out the glass door as Linda's Town Car pulled away. "She said they threw her out because she wore a red dress and harassed Maggie Pearl by telling her that before he died Richard saw her, his first wife, and her family, remembering what they said because she had... thrown a curse on the mayor. Also said heaven to her would be watching the late mayor burn in hell for all eternity."

"Wow. That's what she did, huh? She... cursed him."

The right corner of Dan's mouth curved upward. It was his trademark smile.

"They can't all be home runs, Amelia." Dan put his hand on her back. It was warm and comforting and...thrilling.

"Sorry, I thought maybe she was holding the smoking gun." Amelia leaned into Dan a little.

"Well, I think based on what she said, we can probably rule her out as a suspect. It's looking more and more like George Pilsen's hot dog-vending brother is our man, although he screams he's innocent."

"What about the bodyguards?"

"What about them?"

"Well, disgruntled employees have been known to take out their frustrations on bosses for as long as there have been bosses. You don't think they are worth checking out?"

The sound of shouting and breaking glass stopped their conversation.

Chapter Twelve

Across the street at the Hughes Funeral Chapel, a mob had spilled out onto the sidewalk. Reporters and gawkers were recording the brouhaha as half a dozen men built like linebackers dove into and out of a huddle, throwing fists and screaming obscenities.

"The security is fighting!" Amelia gasped.

"Amelia, I want you to go that way." Dan pointed in the opposite direction of the excitement. "Around the block to where your car is parked and go home."

Something inside the pit of her stomach told her not to argue. Clutching her purse close to her stomach, she moved as quickly as she could without sprinting outright.

People dressed in expensive black clothing seemed to be oozing from the woodwork as she turned the corner. Cars were parked everywhere, most displaying a neon-orange vest worn by city workers on the dashboard or with special plates or stickers indicating to the area tow truck company that they were allowed to park in any fire lane, alley, or handicapped spot.

Quickly getting behind the wheel, Amelia sped out of the parking spot and headed home. Her heart was racing even though she knew the fight wasn't over her. The sight of such big guys throwing punches with their bare fists into the faces of other big guys was disturbing.

What could have caused it? With so many policemen and security, who would take a chance of starting trouble at the funeral of Mayor Pearl? What would the press have to say about this? Was Dan all right?

She recalled how he instructed her to leave and then headed toward the kerfuffle. There had been urgency in his voice. He had the same look on his face as he did when Amelia had told him about the man accosting Meg at the food fest. That man was the primary suspect in a murder right now.

"He obviously knows not to get in between any of those guys," she told the steering wheel. "Dan just doesn't seem like the fighting type." But the image of him pulling those brutes off one another and throwing a couple of punches sent a shiver up her spine. Amelia was afraid to admit the thought made Dan seem damn sexy.

When Amelia finally arrived back home, the sun was starting to set. Just as she was about to shout for Meg, she heard her daughter clopping down the stairs.

"Hi, Mom," she squeaked. "Dad's been trying to reach you. He's called, like, four times."

Amelia kissed her daughter on the head as she passed by on her way to the refrigerator.

"Really? That's funny. My phone must be out of juice," Amelia fibbed. She knew John had been calling. Her phone had vibrated in her purse at least four times while she was driving home, and she was sure it wasn't a telemarketer or Lila or even Dan. "What did he want?"

"He didn't say." Meg pouted her lips at her food options. "But he sounded like he was mad. Did you guys argue again?"

Her daughter didn't look up but grabbed a juice box and shut the door.

"No, honey. And even if we did, you can bet it wasn't about you or your brother. I'll call him back."

Meg walked over to her mom and slipped her arms around her waist, squeezing tight, as she used to when she was just a little girl.

"Well"–Amelia squeezed back–"what is that for?"

"Nothing." Meg's voice was muffled by Amelia's shirt. "Just because Dad can be a jerk sometimes and he doesn't know how hard you work."

"Don't call your father names," Amelia corrected her as she smoothed Meg's hair. "He works hard, too, and is probably just getting stressed out."

It probably is stressful trying to keep up with a twenty-something when you are over fifty. Poor thing. Poor baby.

But Amelia kept her thoughts to herself as usual and would share them only with Lila once they were finally allowed back in the truck to work. As if reading her mind, Meg looked up into her mother's face.

"The cops haven't given us the all clear for work yet, have they?"

Amelia shook her head. "How about sandwiches for supper?"

"Katherine invited me over. Can I go to her house?"

"Sure. Where is your brother?"

"Where else?" Meg jerked her thumb behind her at the basement door. "Probably contacting aliens, hoping they'll beam him aboard the mother ship."

Giving her daughter a playful spank as she went to call Katherine and have dinner with her friend, Amelia opened the basement and called to Adam.

"Do you want sandwiches for supper?"

"Amy invited me to her house for dinner. Can I go?"

Amelia found herself with the next couple of hours alone, and the weight of not being able to finish the Food Fest was nagging at her. When things slipped out of her control, she turned to the one thing that brought her stability and a sense of calm...she baked.

After a quick shower and change of clothes, Amelia looked through her stash in the pantry, found a bottle of unopened honey, apricot preserve, and a bag of shredded coconut.

"When in the world did I buy this?" She turned the bag of coconut over in her hands. "Good thing I did."

With the staples for a moist cake, she started to turn her kitchen into an art studio where she would create a masterpiece. As she sprinkled the flour, sugar, and baking soda into her large mixing bowl, Amelia thought about the day's events one at a time.

Unfortunately, the fact that she had run into her ex-husband stuck in her mind like a tack in a corkboard and just wasn't going to go anywhere until she spoke with him. Turning the oven on to get it warmed up, she decided to get it over with and yank off that Band-Aid in one swift, painful, nerve-wracking yank.

"What in the world were you thinking?" John hissed into the phone.

"Well, hello to you, too." Amelia stared at the counter in front of her, thankful the kids weren't in the house.

"Do you realize how many people saw you and asked me if we had come together? Do you know how that made Jennifer feel?"

"John, are you seriously trying to tell me how my attending the funeral of the mayor of Gary affected *you*? Is that what you came away with?"

"That was Detective Walishovsky with you." He clicked his tongue.

"Dan and I just ran into each other there. He's trying to solve this murder. Of course he'd be at the funeral."

"So *that's* why you had to be there, too." John's voice was like a hot poker.

"What are you talking about?" Amelia was angry. Not just annoyed and not just frustrated, but angry. "I went to see..."

"You went hoping to run into the detective. I know you, Amelia, and..."

Amelia's jaw hit the floor.

"I don't believe you." She chuckled. "Do you really think I am that desperate?"

"I don't know what you are anymore." That comment stuck with Amelia. John didn't know what she was *anymore*. The man she had been married to for sixteen years, who didn't know her while they were together, was complaining that he didn't know her now that they were *not* together.

Like a wave falling over her, Amelia felt her heart stop racing, her fists unclench, and her breath come out in a long, slow stream.

"I've got to go, John. I've got something in the oven."

"Wait," he barked. "Jennifer and I are getting married."

Was it a slap? Was it a punch to the gut Amelia felt? Was it as if a trap door had opened up underneath her feet? No. It was something different.

"Do the kids know?" were the only words she could find.

"Not yet. We were going to tell them when we had them next weekend."

"Okay," Amelia breathed. "Well, I won't say anything. It can be your big surprise."

"You made it very difficult for us to tell anyone today. It was awkward all around." John sounded tired. Jennifer must have given him an earful on the way home.

"Yeah, I'll bet making that big announcement at Mayor Pearl's funeral was ruined by my being there." She almost started to laugh. "Congratulations, John. To both of you."

She pressed the disconnect button and turned back to her baking.

Looking down and grabbing the bottle of honey, Amelia wondered what she was feeling. It was a sort of numbness with a very thin layer of sadness there.

Jennifer was going to be the new Mrs. O'Malley. It was bound to be a major event since Amelia had shouldered the hard part of steering the ship with John going through law school and working for next to nothing trying to make a name for himself. When success and security had finally found them, she had been too busy with kids to realize that her days were numbered.

"Live and learn, I guess," she said soothingly to herself while squirting a healthy dose of honey into the batter. Crying was an option. The pit that had formed in her stomach at hearing the news from John wanted a way out. It pushed and tumbled inside her, inching its way closer and closer to her eyes, but she stopped it there.

Amelia didn't want to get back together with John. She was actually enjoying her new life. The freedom, the independence.

The Pink Cupcake had carved out a place for her in the world. She was no longer John O'Malley's wife. She hadn't been for quite some time. She was Amelia Harley, businesswoman and single mom. Those were badges she was proud to wear.

"So why do you feel like you want to crumple to the floor and cry like a baby?" Her eyes glistened a little. "Because it still hurts."

Having promised herself she wouldn't cry, Amelia went to the sink, pulled down a coffee cup from the cabinet, filled it with lukewarm water from the tap, and drank it down.

"Maybe that should have been whiskey," she joked, instantly thinking of Lila. She dialed her number, held her breath, and waited for her friend to answer.

"Hey." Lila's voice was cheery as always. "Are we back to work?"

Amelia lost it. She spilled the whole horrible story, crying like a dumped teenager and wiping her nose on the sleeve of her shirt.

"I'll be right over," was all Lila said. Within twenty minutes, she was letting herself in the front door with a bottle of wine in one hand and a bouquet of flowers in the other.

"I feel so stupid, Lila," she blubbered. "I don't want John back. I guess I just..."

"You thought there might be a longer grieving period."

Amelia nodded, taking a sip of the white wine they had quickly opened and going back to stirring her batter.

"And if the Food Fest hadn't turned out to be such a bust, I probably would have offered to throw them an engagement party." Amelia laughed.

"Let's not get crazy," Lila interjected, holding her right hand up in front of her. "That is probably what's got you more upset than anything. Because if we were working and you needed cupcakes, your mind would be on that, not roaming free like a grazing cow."

"Something like that." Amelia laughed. Lila was right. It wasn't John she was upset about—it was that her business was being severely dented by this whole scandal with the late mayor, and there wasn't a darn thing Amelia could do about it.

The conversation drifted from the news of John and Jennifer's engagement, to the

Food Fest, to lunch with Gavin from the Philly Cheese Steak truck, to the visit to the funeral, and Dan.

By the time they got to the topic of Detective Walishovsky, the bottle of wine was empty and piping-hot honey-apricot cupcakes with almond frosting were cooling on the counter.

"They smell good," Lila said encouragingly. "Probably because they are sweetened with your tears."

"Right?" Amelia chuckled. "They'll never turn out this good again unless I make them while going through some tragedy. That's what I'll call them. Tragedy cupcakes."

"Disappointment cakes," Lila added, laughing loudly.

"Cakes of Regret!" Amelia was holding her stomach, she was laughing so hard, until she saw her phone light up and the wind-chime ringer go off.

"It's John," Lila said teasingly. "He wants to know if you'll make the wedding cake. At cost, of course."

Amelia let out a sarcastic burst of laughter but quickly composed herself, her hand going to the back of her neck to smooth her hair down.

"Hi, Dan." She put her index finger to her lips, to which Lila nodded and winked. "What's going on?"

Lila could hear the detective's serious voice and watched Amelia smile and nod.

"Sure. I'd be happy to help." She looked down at her casual clothes—baggy jeans and a long-sleeved shirt—and shrugged. "Okay, twenty minutes is fine. See you shortly."

When Amelia pressed the disconnect button on her phone, she looked up to see Lila already grabbing her purse and pulling out her keys, a devilish smirk on her face.

"What are you and the detective up to?"

"Oh, it's really nothing." Amelia shook her head and took a cupcake from the cooling rack, handing it to Lila. "He's going on a stakeout and asked if I wanted to go along. You know, I went before, and it was kind of fun, so I guess..."

Lila took her cupcake.

"Well, I'm glad he's driving since you had two rather large glasses of wine."

"Oh, gosh." Amelia waved her hand in the air rather flamboyantly. "I'm fine. I had more wine than that once and baked dour fozen brownies without burning one."

"Dour fozen?"

"Four dozen! Oh, Lila, you are a bad influence!" They laughed as Amelia hugged her friend and watched as she climbed into her car and pulled out of the driveway.

Shutting the door quickly, Amelia ran upstairs to brush her teeth, put on a little lip gloss, and change into a different shirt, remembering she had used her sleeve as a handkerchief just a short while ago.

After settling on a red sweater that looked cute with her dungarees, Amelia bolted downstairs and slipped into her gym shoes, grabbed her surveillance gear, and managed to stuff it all in her bag just as the doorbell rang.

Grabbing two cupcakes, she opened the door, looked up, and gasped.

Chapter Thirteen

"What happened to your face?" She nearly dropped her things as she reached up to touch Dan's cheek, where a swollen bump was proceeding to turn a deep purple.

"I was born with it," Dan said teasingly as he escorted her to the car.

After she had left the funeral, Dan had had to dive into the fight that had broken out in front of the funeral home.

"It was just a lucky punch. You should see the other guy," he joked.

"Did you put any ice on it?"

"I haven't had time." He sort of smirked, but it looked as though it hurt to do even that. "Assaulting an officer is against the law. I've been at the station with a few of the guys you said you overheard talking."

Amelia raised her eyebrows and turned around to look over the top of her shoulder at Dan.

"Ever hear of a bar called The Boss Bar?"

"Nope."

"Well, that's where we are heading."

"Why?"

"Because that is where the security guards hang out when they have time off. And two of the three you overheard were heading that way."

"Why would they tell you that after you arrested them?" Amelia was enthralled. John and Jennifer were completely forgotten.

"In order to get off the hook, they offered some information. It seems that their free ride ran out of gas." Dan stretched his fingers against the steering wheel, and Amelia saw they were swollen, too. "No one from the Pearl camp sent anyone to bail them out or get them out of trouble. So, for the first time in several years, they were on their own to clean up their mess.

Guys like that, guys who are easily led and manipulated...they are faithful to no one."

"So what did they say?"

"It wasn't what they said—it was what one of them didn't say."

Amelia leaned in, looking from the windshield to Dan and back again.

"It was the weird bald guy, wasn't it? The bald guy?"

"No." Dan tightened his lips together. "Chuck DeLuca. He's got blond hair, his eyes are kind of..."

"Chinese?" Amelia blurted out. "Sorry, that's not very PC. Lila and I had some wine before you came over. I'm afraid I'm a little more brazen than usual."

Dan gave Amelia a sideways glance as if he didn't approve. "Miss Harley, I'm shocked at you."

"Oh, hush and tell me what he said."

"The fight was between these three guys that had been protecting the mayor. Jones—the bald guy—and Lamar, the black guy, said that DeLuca started it. He had been on detail with the mayor for several years. According to Jones and Lamar, the mayor treated DeLuca like a redheaded stepchild. That guy couldn't do anything right."

"So why didn't he fire him?"

"Don't know," Dan mumbled.

They drove into Bridgeport in silence. Amelia watched as the buildings slowly morphed into smaller, cozier blue-collar mom-and-pop establishments. There were VFWs and corner grocery stores. The streets were well lit and clean.

The homes were just a few steps past modest, with long driveways and simply manicured laws.

"There's our place." Dan pointed ahead to a green-and-orange neon sign that glared The Boss Bar. It was on a corner. The windows were darkened and couldn't be seen into even at this hour of the night when the sun was down.

Loitering outside were a couple of hulking forms shuffling their feet, smoking cigarettes, and talking to each other.

"Are you sure about this place?" Amelia asked.

"Yeah. My contact said DeLuca showed up in there just a little after the brawl. He's been there ever since."

"Yikes." Amelia grimaced. The idea of drinking for that many hours made her stomach flip. Suddenly, she remembered her cupcakes. "Hungry?" she asked, presenting Dan with one.

"Well, it'll cost me a few more miles on the treadmill, but okay."

"This is a new recipe. If you don't like it, don't hold back."

Dan pulled around a corner so he could creep up an alley that was right across from the bar, where he could see who was coming and going. He took a bite of the cupcake just as he raised his binoculars to his eyes.

Amelia, with a cupcake in one hand and her own binoculars in the other, followed suit.

Just as they took a bite, the suspect, DeLuca, leaned out the door and began yelling and cussing at the men who were on the sidewalk. He was screaming at them so loudly that Amelia could hear the obscenities through the rolled-up windows.

"What in the world?"

Dan watched as DeLuca went back into the bar, slamming the door shut.

"You wait here," Dan said, getting out of the driver's side and quickly making his way up to the entrance of the bar and disappearing inside.

Amelia sat still for a few minutes until curiosity got the best of her.

"It's dangerous," she mumbled, licking the frosting from her lips. "Dan said stay put. I should listen. These guys are big and...big." She watched as the door flew open and DeLuca came stumbling out alone.

"Where is he?" Crumbs fell from her mouth as she spoke. Dan did not follow DeLuca out of the bar.

"He's getting away. He's fleeing, sort of." She watched as DeLuca stumbled and staggered his way down the sidewalk, using the side of the building to hold himself up every couple of steps.

Without thinking, Amelia slowly got out of the car and began to follow DeLuca as he drunkenly wove his way back and forth along the sidewalk. Quietly, she hurried on tiptoe to get closer to him.

"This is it! I'll kill you," DeLuca grumbled, each comment becoming more and more vulgar. "I've done it before. That's right! I've done it, and I'll do it to you, too."

Amelia hung back, hopping from shadow to shadow until DeLuca stopped and stood stone still in the middle of the sidewalk.

She froze. Had he heard her footsteps? Heard her breathing?

It was cool outside. The air smelled different from the street Amelia lived on. It had a metallic, industrial smell to it that reminded Amelia that she was way out of her element. To turn tail and run now would give her position away. And just because the guy couldn't walk didn't mean he couldn't run if he felt he had to.

Finally, DeLuca began walking again. He rounded a corner and stood at the bottom of a stoop to a nice three-flat home. Watching, Amelia saw in the light from the streetlamp DeLuca pulling a gun from the inside of his coat.

He swayed uneasily and pointed the gun across the street. Shooting sounds could be heard coming from his mouth as he took aim at houses, garbage cans, and a couple of parked cars. Pulling himself up the stairs by the railing, DeLuca kept the gun in one hand while he fumbled with his keys in the other hand.

Tripping and nearly falling in the door, DeLuca made it inside and slammed the door shut, his keys still dangling from the doorknob.

"He's going to kill himself." Amelia felt panic rise up from her feet. Without warning, images of her children surfaced in her mind. DeLuca was someone's son. Wouldn't she hope that if one of her children were in this kind of pain, someone would step in to help?

Pulling her cell phone from her pocket, Amelia quickly dialed Dan's number. He didn't answer.

"Dan. I'm at 20045 Batton Street. It's just around from the bar. I followed that DeLuca guy to his house, and I think...I'm sure he's going to kill himself. He pulled a gun out of his pocket on the sidewalk. He left his keys in the door. He's so drunk, heaven knows what he's going to do up there."

The voice mail cut her off.

Chapter Fourteen

Amelia couldn't deny her motherly instinct. She had to do something. If she waited for Dan, it could be too late. "He's someone's son." She worried as she shoved her fear aside and marched up the stairs. Slowly, she turned the keys in the doorknob, heard the click, and pushed the door open.

The home had the distinct smell of a home different from hers. It wasn't foul, but it wasn't sweet either. It was a mixture of someone else's habits, someone else's taste in foods, different cleaning products and soaps.

"Hello?" she called, not too loud for fear of scaring DeLuca into accidentally discharging his weapon that she was sure was pointed at his own head. "Hello? You left your keys in your door."

There was no answer except the tick-tick-tick of a clock somewhere in the darkness. The curtains were drawn as she went up two steps to enter the living room. A recliner, of course, was front and center in front of a large flat-screen television. A sectional took up the far wall. As her eyes adjusted, Amelia could make out several beer bottles on the floor. The sweet smell of stale beer could also be detected now that she noticed it.

"Hello? Is anyone home?" Amelia cleared her throat. "You left your keys..."

"Amelia?"

Turning with a quick yelp, Amelia whirled around to see the familiar silhouette of Dan standing in the doorway. He had his gun raised and pointing toward the ceiling.

"Are you insane?" he hissed.

"Both of you can hold it right there!" came the slurred voice of Chuck DeLuca, who was sitting on an ottoman in an almost completely black shadow. "Drop that gun, pal."

Dan set the gun down and raised his hands.

"You left your keys in the door. I just happened to notice you when you came in and..."

"You mean, when you were following me," DeLuca slurred. "I saw you all the way back at the bar. Not very stealthy."

"No. I'm not," Amelia confessed. "I saw you with your gun, and I thought..."

"You thought what?" He slowly stood up. "Just shut that door behind you, partner. I don't want to be disturbed anymore tonight."

"I thought, well, that you were going to kill yourself and..."

"Kill myself?" A phlegmy, drunken laugh came out of him. "I don't think so. But I could kill two intruders who broke into my house. By the time the cops arrived, I'd have all the evidence cleaned up."

"Evidence?" Dan mumbled. "It'll be pretty hard to dispose of two bodies, one the chief detective for Gary PD, the other a mother of two with no history of crimes."

"Shut up, *Detective*. I wasn't talking about *that* evidence. Hell, I could leave you both lying on the floor to bleed to death. No one would blame me for shooting two strangers in my house."

Amelia looked at Dan in the darkness and wanted to cry again. What had she done? She'd entered a strange man's house. What did she think the guy was going to do?

"I thought you were going to hurt yourself," Amelia said pleadingly.

"Shut up," DeLuca snapped, but it didn't seem as if he were talking to Amelia. "I'll handle this. Like I handle it all. I handle it all." His breathing started to become erratic, and in the pale light peeking from the drawn curtains, Amelia could see DeLuca's forehead glistening with sweat.

"It's over, and you won't feel a thing. I told you, you won't. You won't!"

"Just calm down," Dan said soothingly.

"You shut your mouth! That's all I ever hear from you!" DeLuca wasn't talking to Amelia or Dan but some other demon that was in the room tormenting him. He spewed out a string of horrific profanities. His body jerked and twisted, and all the while he held the gun on both of them. One false move, one squeeze of the trigger, and everything would be over.

"You think I'm going to listen to you now? Ha! You're dead! You're dead, and you're not coming back. I beat you! You fat...crooked... cheating piece of dog...! I killed you!"

Amelia's mind tried to focus. She thought of her children. That was all she ever thought of. That was why she did what she did. Payback couldn't be a bullet in the gut!

"Mr. DeLuca?" she whispered. "Can you put the gun down?"

He stopped, and she felt his eyes boring into her. Bad move, Amelia. Such a bad move.

"How do you know my name?"

"I told her," Dan interrupted and came up the step behind Amelia. Carefully, almost as if he were showing her a slow dance move, Dan positioned himself between her and DeLuca. "Mr. DeLuca, you've had enough to drink today. Put the gun down, and we can talk."

"I'm not talking to you. You're dead. I'm dead. We're all dead. But my soul will live. I'm not going to hell because I killed you. No matter what you say." Then DeLuca began to not just cry, but sob pitifully. "You made me do those things, and I didn't want to. I didn't want to! But whatever the mayor wants, right? Just take the money, you said! A coward like me! Just take the money!"

Before she could focus on what was happening, Amelia saw a rush of movement and felt a hand against her shoulder, then she fell down the two steps, losing her balance and landing on her fanny. The gun went off.

Chapter Fifteen

There were punches being landed and shuffling on the floor as furniture was knocked out of the way. Grunting and more swearing came from DeLuca as he tried to stand up, but before she could get to her feet, Amelia heard Dan and the click-click-click of handcuffs.

"You have...the right to remain...silent..." He finished the Miranda rights in gasps and finally stood up.

When he turned on a light, his eyes squinted. Amelia was sure he was more than angry with her, but when he saw her sprawled on the floor, he quickly reached his hand down to her.

"Are you okay?"

Nodding, Amelia took his hand and got to her feet. Only when she turned and looked at poor Mr. Chuck DeLuca panting and weeping on the floor did she see what he was looking at.

Across from him, covering the entire wall, were newspaper clippings. Every article was something about Mayor Pearl and the variety of dealings he had his hands in. There was a land grab in the Southwestern suburb of Minooka where the mayor planned a new airport. The residents were opposed to it. Each article had red markings on it. A name circled. Gertrude Bullerdick. It was circled and written all over the collage of articles DeLuca had taped to the wall.

"Chuck. Who is Gertrude?" Dan asked, careful to only touch the newspapers with the tip of the pen he pulled from his pocket.

Rolling over onto his back, the large man sat up, and Amelia was positive he was smiling.

"She was just a nice old lady." He grinned as tears rolled down his cheeks. "She lived in Minooka her whole life. She didn't want to move. But Richard..." He swallowed hard. "He wanted her to change her mind. He offered her money and a new house free and clear if she'd just get off the land."

"You mean Mayor Pearl?"

"Who else do you think I mean?" He began to hiss and rant again as if his mind had snapped. "She was only thirty-two."

"Who was?"

"Mrs. Bullerdick's daughter."

"Where is she?"

"I took a payoff. I didn't know that's what it was for. But I knew he'd get away with it. He paid off my house. He bought my car. All I had to do was do as he said. That was it. It sounded so easy..."

Amelia put her hand to her stomach and reached out to Dan, who told her backup was on the way.

He took her outside, as Chuck DeLuca seemed content to just sit on the floor handcuffed. The fresh air made everything stop spinning, and Amelia sat down on the stoop.

"Is it just me or...did he just confess to doing something really bad to someone."

"Amelia, do you have any idea what a dangerous thing you just did?" Dan's eyes filled with tears. "What would I have told

Adam and Meg if..." His words stuck in his throat. Coughing, he took her hand in his. "If something would have happened to you?"

Swallowing hard, Amelia didn't try to explain her reason for taking such a stupid risk. It was stupid, and Dan was right. She just hated the idea of someone feeling that much pain, feeling that alone. Maybe part of her was trying to rescue herself from feeling so alone and so abandoned.

"I'm sorry, Dan." She squeezed his hand back. The image of his bruised face tore at her heart. Gently, she put her hand up to his cheek. "I'm sorry."

Before she could stop herself, Amelia pulled Dan's hand to her chest, leaned forward, and kissed him. Her heart flooded with adrenaline as she felt his other hand slip around her waist and pull her closer to him.

It wasn't appropriate, with the suspect of a murder handcuffed inside the house they were sitting in front of, but it felt right. She inhaled the smell of his skin, felt the tears that had rolled down his cheek, and enjoyed the strength in his arms as they tightened around her. Her mind pushed out everything else, and she felt at ease in this moment, in this place, with this man.

Amelia couldn't tell how much time had gone by. Before she realized it, the sound of sirens was echoing down the alleys and bouncing off the buildings, getting louder as they got closer. Pulling away from his lips was like the last bite of dessert or the end of a favorite song.

Feeling her cheeks blazing red, Amelia looked up at Dan. His blue eyes twinkled, looking pleased with this new development, and the right side of his mouth curled into that devilish smirk Amelia found irresistible.

"I'll have one of the officers take you home after you give a statement." He stood from the steps, helping her get to her feet.

"Will I get you in trouble? Tagging along on a stakeout then letting myself into a strange person's house."

Dan leaned down, lifted Amelia's chin with his finger, and kissed her on the lips.

"Just tell the truth. It'll be all right." He leaned back and winked at her as he went back up the stairs to check on the suspect.

Chuck DeLuca was sitting quietly on the floor where Dan had left him, tears streaming down his face. The police arrived along with an ambulance.

While Amelia was telling one of the uniformed officers what had happened, she saw them wheeling DeLuca out on a stretcher, strapped down tightly, his face much calmer than it had been.

"When I saw the gun and how drunk he was, I was afraid he was going to kill himself. That's why I went into his house." The officer looked at Amelia as if she had all of a sudden broken into song to tell her story. "I know it was dumb. But he's someone's son. I have a son. I'd hope someone would help him if he needed it." She looked down at her hands.

Perhaps she should be embarrassed, maybe even ashamed at her actions. There was no telling what kind of ticking bomb DeLuca was or where his mind might have been when she stepped foot in his house. But she had her reason, and to her it made perfect sense.

Shortly after DeLuca was carted away, the press showed up. Dan pulled a uniformed officer aside, pointed to Amelia, and gave him some fast instructions. The man nodded and smiled as he approached Amelia.

"Dan said you needed a lift home."

"If it's no bother."

"None at all. I'm six months from retirement, and the less excitement I'm around, the better." The officer led Amelia to his squad car. She climbed in and told him her address, to which the officer said he had a high school buddy who lived in the same subdivision.

When she got home, the kids were waiting up and wound up tighter than clocks.

"Where've you been?" they asked scoldingly. "We've been worried sick."

"I'm sorry." Amelia smiled through her exhaustion.

"You've never heard of a telephone? You couldn't call?" Meg shook her finger at her mother.

"We almost called the police." Adam scoffed, folding his arms in front of his chest.

"I was with Dan. He was on a stakeout and asked..."

"I've heard enough!" Meg put up her hand as if she were trying to stop traffic.

"And here I thought Dan was a responsible young man."

"Meg and I will need some time to decide on your punishment," Adam said, putting his arm around his sister. "We're not mad. Just...disappointed."

"Are you kidding me?" Amelia rolled her eyes and shook her head. "You guys won't believe the night I've had."

She looked at Adam, who was trying hard not to laugh at the performance he and his sister were putting on. Amelia thought of why she went into Chuck DeLuca's house again, and tears surfaced in her eyes, but she bit them back.

"I'm sorry. You guys are right. I would tan your hides if you didn't call me. I should have called you. Everything happened so fast, I didn't even realize what time it was until it was way late."

She walked into the kitchen and saw the remaining four cupcakes had been devoured.

"What did you think of my honey apricot cupcakes?"

"They were delicious," Meg snapped then looked up to the ceiling as if there were something of interest up there to distract her from pretending to be furious at her mother. Finally, she looked at her mom and giggled. "So are you going to tell us what happened, or do we have to wait until it's all over the news?"

The kids took a seat around the kitchen table while Amelia pulled a jug of milk out of the fridge and poured them each a glass. She began with Lila stopping by and ended with the ride home in the squad car. She left out the kiss between her and Dan. But her heart fluttered at the thought of it.

"Well, I think I've got an idea what Mom's punishment should be." Adam kept his face completely stoic, making Meg laugh.

"Do tell, Adam," she urged him.

"She should write a blog about why you should always call if you're going to be late and tell everyone that she made her children worry and get premature gray hair."

"Yes," Meg concurred. "That is a punishment that fits the crime."

Amelia looked at her children as if they had each just grown an eyeball in the middle of their foreheads.

"I'll expect to read it on The Pink Cupcake website within the next three days, since it takes you that long to update your blog," Adam said teasingly.

"And it better be done, or else that will be the last time you see that Dan Walishovsky." Meg stared down her nose, desperately holding in her giggles.

"What do you guys think of Dan?"

"Well, after tonight, I'm not sure what I think of that hooligan." Adam made his sister crack up.

"I like him," Meg replied in between laughs. "And I think he likes you."

"What makes you say that?" Amelia asked, smiling at her daughter.

"You know, he always makes a point to stop by and check on you, and he eats all your cupcakes, and he looks at you when you're not looking at him."

"Yeah, that's the big one," Adam added. "He's stealthy that way."

Amelia swallowed hard and nodded, smiling a little.

"Okay, well, it's late. We all should get to bed now that everyone is accounted for." Amelia didn't want to talk about Dan anymore. She wanted to just lie down in bed and quietly sort through her thoughts and feelings and see what everything added up to.

After they finished their milk and put their glasses in the sink, Meg said good night and made her way upstairs. Adam waited for his mom to stand up and start turning the lights off.

"I think Dan is a good guy, Mom," he mused. "I think he's the kind of guy who would appreciate you. You should have a guy like that."

Amelia smiled and rubbed her son's hair.

"Thank you, baby." She pulled him close to her and squeezed him tight.

"I'm not a baby anymore, Mom."

"What are you talking about? You'll always be my baby." She kissed his cheek and watched as he didn't wipe it off, as he might have done when he was ten or twelve. Instead, he smiled and headed toward the basement.

"But don't think this gets you out of your punishment. Three days." He shook his finger at her.

Amelia clicked her tongue and headed upstairs. As soon as her head hit the pillow, she was dead asleep.

Chapter Sixteen

It was barely twenty-four hours before the news of Chuck DeLuca's arrest in the murder of Mayor Richard M. Pearl flashed across every local news station. Dan managed to keep Amelia's name out of it and instead had her referred to as a Good Samaritan who stumbled upon DeLuca in a severely drunken state and tried to help him.

As it turned out, once DeLuca was removed from the premises, the police found an extensive search history of poisons on his computer as well as residue in his kitchen and dining room for the same poison that had killed the mayor.

Dan had come to Amelia's house as soon as he was off duty, bringing hamburgers for everyone.

Meg and Adam took their food and went into the front room to watch some sci-fi movie with aliens and spaceships while Amelia and Dan sat at the kitchen table.

"It's a lot sadder than just a guy who went off the deep end," he mumbled to Amelia while helping her set the table. "Chuck DeLuca was suffering from severe post-traumatic stress disorder."

"From what?" Amelia's eyes were wide.

"Everyone knew how corrupt Mayor Pearl was, but there is a difference between taking money for a few special jobs and actually killing someone to get your way. According to DeLuca, the mayor rescued him from a dangerous life bouncing at some of the more insidious clubs in Gary."

Dan took a seat and rolled up his sleeves.

"DeLuca worked as a bouncer, used steroids, and was heavily into partying when Pearl 'discovered' him. According to DeLuca, he was partying with a girl who overdosed at an after-party that the mayor just happened to have people at. They took care of the girl. DeLuca had a permanent job working for one of the most corrupt mayors in US history. They cleaned him up, dried him out, put him in a suit, and in their eyes, owned him lock, stock, and barrel."

"But why would he have PTSD?"

"Well, you and I know that that kind of deal never comes for free." He took a big bite of his burger and wiped his mouth with a napkin. "DeLuca said the mayor had enough on him to pin the party girl's death on him if he didn't play ball. What else could he do? And in return for keeping quiet about the girl, Mayor Pearl, man of the people, pushed DeLuca to the brink."

Amelia stopped chewing and leaned forward, engrossed in the story.

"According to the other guards, the fellows you saw with him at the funeral, Mayor Pearl took a special pleasure out of harassing DeLuca. He called him every name under the sun, insulted him at every turn. And DeLuca couldn't do a damn thing about it. The mayor owned his house, his car, his soul."

"He couldn't quit?"

"Not without the mayor either turning information over to the DA to get him tossed in jail for this mystery girl's death or..."

"Or what?"

"Or blaming him for the death of Gertrude Bullerdick's daughter. The problem was, the girl who he thought died of an overdose was never found. There was never any report of a missing girl, an overdose victim, and because it was a one-night kind of thing, DeLuca couldn't even be sure of her name. But he believed the mayor and his people who told him that they had 'handled' that situation. He believed that they had saved him from jail. In his mind, he owed them."

Dan stopped for a moment and knitted his eyebrows.

"The problem now was that Gertrude Bullerdick's daughter was real. She had a mother and friends and coworkers. She was an innocent person."

"What did he do?"

Taking a deep breath, Dan described the interrogation at the hospital.

The room the police questioned DeLuca in was barely private. Just a thin blue curtain separated him from a car accident victim on one side and an intoxicated woman who had fallen down the steps at the commuter train station on the other.

The rest of the emergency room bustled and buzzed like a wasp nest that had been poked with a stick. Dan had been pacing back and forth at the end of the small cubicle, waiting for the doctor and nurses to give him the all clear to talk to his suspect. They bustled around DeLuca, shouting instructions and forcing a tube down his throat and into his stomach to pump over eight hours' worth of alcohol out of it.

Finally, when they had forcibly sobered him up, Dan stepped up to the bed and looked at him. He was handcuffed to the bed railing. His body was covered in sweat, and yet there was a peaceful aura to him.

"Hello, Detective," he mumbled, averting his eyes.

"Mr. DeLuca, I just want to ask you a few questions."

"I did it." He finally lifted his chin and looked Dan in the eyes. "I killed Richard Pearl." He didn't smile or laugh. The crazy babblings of the night before had vanished.

"How did you do that, Chuck?"

"With arsenic. The guy ate everything. It wasn't hard to find an opportunity to do it. The only hard part was finding a venue, you know, a way to get 'er done without having it come back to me." He started to laugh then stopped, rubbing his throat. The tube had probably torn it up a little and made it sensitive.

"What's funny about that, Chuck?"

"The funny part is that I made it come back to me. Had I been like Pearl, had I not had a conscience, had I slept on enough rolls of money from dealings like the Minooka Airport deal, maybe I could have held it together. Maybe I could have let Pilson's brother take the rap."

Chuck DeLuca went on to describe the kind of conditions he had worked under as Mayor Pearl's bodyguard. The constant verbal abuse and unreasonable demands were enough to drive anyone to the edge. At least four times a week, DeLuca was called in the middle of the night to bring the man some kind of delivery. Sometimes it was money from an informant. Sometimes it was drugs. Sometimes it was confidential paperwork. Sometimes it was McDonald's. Every time he entered the room of a "private meeting," Pearl would address him as a part of the female body – in the crudest word he knew. He questioned his manhood, criticized his abilities, and was just mean. Mean for sport. And when the option to quit wasn't even there, DeLuca had felt he was already living out a life sentence.

"It was hell."

Dan was writing everything down in his small notebook. But when DeLuca said these words, he stopped and looked at the man. The suspect had tears in his eyes that he went to wipe away but was stopped by the metal clank of the cuffs against the bed railing. He used his other hand.

"I just couldn't do it. I couldn't keep quiet, not about this." He shook his head, again unable to look at Dan. "I kept seeing Gertrude Bullerdick's daughter's face. She kept telling me what to do. She said I needed to turn myself in and confess to everything. She said she'd never leave until I did. Detective, do you believe a man can change his ways?"

Dan looked back at his notebook. He was used to criminals having a change of heart after they had been caught. This was nothing new to him, and he kept his hard edge while Chuck DeLuca, the man who would now forever be known as the man who poisoned Richard M. Pearl, tried to clear his conscience.

"I think anything is possible, Mr. DeLuca."

"I think a man can," DeLuca mumbled, a hint of singsongy happiness in his tone. "Because I don't see her anymore." He smiled widely.

Those were the last words Dan got out of DeLuca. He informed him of his rights again, said a public defender might be paying him a visit and that if he kept his story the same, he might get a lesser sentence. Dan also promised to make sure the judge knew he had been more than cooperative.

Dan took a sip from the large paper cup he brought with the food.

"Like 'The Tell-Tale Heart,' what he did was tearing him apart inside. In his own twisted way, he thought the way to even the playing field wasn't to fess up but to put an end to Mayor Pearl once and for all."

"That's sad."

"That's nothing. DeLuca isn't alone. Dozens of people are coming to his defense, stating that they had horrific experiences at the hands of Mayor Richard M. Pearl, too."

"What does that mean for you?"

"It looks like this guy might get a plea deal based on the fact he might be mentally unhinged. Like an abused spouse who wanted to leave, but where would he go? The mayor had too much on him and assumed he was too afraid to ever go against him."

Taking a sip of her own drink, Amelia couldn't help but think of Maggie. She seemed like such a nice person. Amelia believed she really loved the mayor. But what was that saying—a man could read fine literature, listen to Mozart, and have a refined taste in wine while every morning getting up to go to work at Auschwitz or something like that. People had double lives.

"There are absolutely no winners in this case." Amelia hummed before taking another bite of her burger.

"No." Dan took another big bite while watching Amelia. She was swishing her French fries in some ketchup when she looked up to find him staring at her. Blushing, she gave him a roll of her eyes.

"Sorry the whole thing ruined your first experience with the Gary Food Fest."

"Thanks for bringing that up." She slouched. "I think I might have lost my appetite."

"You'll recover." Dan patted her hand, slipped his underneath hers, lifted it to his lips, and kissed it gently. Goose bumps ran up her arm, and Amelia smiled, happy in her embarrassment. They finished their lunch discussing another case that had been nagging at Dan for several weeks. It was a missing person.

Before he left to shower and change his clothes at his own bachelor apartment, Dan said good-bye to Adam and Meg. Amelia walked him slowly to the front door.

"Well, don't work too hard." She slipped her delicate hand into his.

Dan looked down at her and took a step closer. He still had that serious look on his face, but Amelia was proud of the fact that she could sense the smile in his eyes. Blinking up at him, she stepped back a little, leaning casually against the wall.

"So," he purred. "Do you mind if I give you a call later?" He placed his arm over her head, cornering her between him and the wall.

"No, Detective. I don't mind at all."

Amelia stood on her tiptoes to meet him halfway. For a few moments, they kissed quietly. Finally, letting out a deep breath, Dan leaned back and gave Amelia one last peck on the top of her head and a wink as he walked out the door.

* * *

The Pink Cupcake was finally released from quarantine. They had missed almost the entire Food Fest event. The remaining time would have been long enough for the ovens to warm up before they'd have to shut them down again.

Amelia drove The Pink Cupcake back home, happy to have it back in her driveway. As soon as she walked in the door, her phone started buzzing. It was Officer Darcy Miller, her favorite catering customer. Amelia wondered if she was making good on her offer for another catering job.

"There is a string of retirements coming up, and you know, if we were to do a party for each guy, it's going to run each officer a couple hundred dollars each. Crazy as it may seem, being a public servant doesn't pay all that great."

"None of the jobs that require actual hard work ever do," Amelia joked.

Darcy explained there was going to be a giant party for about five hundred to seven hundred and fifty people at The Sabre Room restaurant. It would be about a month from today, and they could pay her more than her normal fee if she could personalize the cupcakes for the three retirees and their specific duties.

"Do you think you can do it?"

Quickly doing the math in her head, Amelia figured it would cut the damage done by the Gary Food Fest debacle in half.

"Yes." She smiled confidently. "I can do it."

Recipe 1: Honey Apricot Cupcakes

Makes 12

Ingredients:
- 1 1/4 cup flour
- 1 cup apricot puree
- 1/3 cup vegetable oil
- 1/3 cup honey
- 2/3 cup sugar
- 1/4 cup milk
- 1 tsp vanilla extract
- 1/2 tsp baking soda
- 1/2 tsp baking powder
- 1/4 tsp cinnamon
- 1/4 tsp ground cloves
- 1/4 tsp nutmeg

Almond Butter Frosting:

- 2 cups icing sugar
- 1 cup almond butter
- 1/2 cup butter, softened
- 3 Tbsp milk or whipping cream, or as needed

Stir apricot, vegetable oil, milk, honey, sugar, and vanilla in a bowl. Sift in flour, baking soda, baking powder, and spices. Mix gently. Divide among cupcake liners (about 3/4 full each). Bake for 20 minutes at 350 degrees F.

Almond Butter Frosting:

Beat butter and almond butter with an electric mixer. Slowly add in sugar. When frosting gets thick, add milk by the tablespoon until frosting is thick and spreadable. Beat for at least 3 minutes.

Spread on cooled cupcakes.

Recipe 2: Coconut Cherry Cupcakes

Makes 12

Ingredients for Cupcake:
- 1 cup sugar
- 3/4 cups self-rising flour
- 6 Tbsp all-purpose flour
- 8 oz unsalted butter, softened
- 2 large eggs, at room temperature
- 1/2 cup light coconut milk
- 1/4 cup shredded coconut
- 1/4 cup sour cream
- 1 tsp coconut extract
- 4 oz frozen pitted cherries

Coconut Buttercream Icing:

• 4 oz unsalted butter, softened

• 3/4 cup icing sugar

• 1/4 tsp coconut extract

• 1/2 cup shredded coconut to decorate (optional)

Preheat oven to 350 degrees F. Line a 12-cupcake tray with liners. Combine flours and shredded coconut in a small bowl and set aside.

Cream butter in a large bowl on medium speed with an electric mixer. Slowly add sugar and beat until fluffy, around 2 minutes. Beat in eggs one at a time. Add coconut extract. Add the dry ingredients, alternating with the coconut milk and sour cream. Don't overbeat.

Cut cherries in half and add to batter. Scoop batter into cupcake liners, around 3/4 full. Bake for around 20 minutes, or until they spring back when pressed.

Cool the cupcakes in the tray for 10 minutes. Remove from tray and cool completely on a wire rack before icing.

Coconut Buttercream Icing:

Cream butter in a large bowl on medium speed with an electric mixer until smooth. Add the icing sugar and coconut extract until combined.

Ice cooled cupcakes with buttercream. Decorate with shredded coconut.

About the Author

Harper Lin is the USA TODAY bestselling author of 6 cozy mystery series including *The Patisserie Mysteries* and *The Cape Bay Cafe Mysteries*.

When she's not reading or writing mysteries, she loves going to yoga classes, hiking, and hanging out with her family and friends.

www.HarperLin.com

49646380R00119

Made in the USA
San Bernardino, CA
31 May 2017